Returning to A

Dorien Ross

CITY LIGHTS

FIC

© 1995 by Dorien Ross
All Rights Reserved
10 9 8 7 6 5 4 3 2 1

Cover design: John Miller/BigFish Books
Front cover: Photo (center) of Diego del Gastor by Bill Davidson
Book design: Nancy J. Peters
Typography: Harvest Graphics

Library of Congress Cataloging-in-Publication Data

Ross, Dorien.
    Returning to "A" / Dorien Ross.
        p.   cm.
    ISBN 0-87286-306-9 (hardcover). — ISBN 0-87286-307-7 (pbk.)
    1. Americans—Travel—Spain—Fiction.   2. Teenage girls
—Spain—Fiction.   3. Jewish girls—Spain—Fiction.   4. Guitarists
—Spain—Fiction.   5. Flamenco music—Fiction.   I. Title.
PS3568.084322R47   1995
813'.54—dc20   95-31001
                                                             CIP

City Lights Books are available to bookstores through our primary
distributor: Subterranean Company. P. O. Box 160, 265 S. 5th St.,
Monroe, OR 97456. 503-847-5274. Toll-free orders 800-274-7826.
FAX 503-847-6018. Our books are also available through library jobbers
and regional distributors. For personal orders and catalogs, please write
to City Lights Books, 261 Columbus Avenue, San Francisco CA 94133.

CITY LIGHTS BOOKS are edited by Lawrence Ferlinghetti and
Nancy J. Peters and published at the City Lights Bookstore,
261 Columbus Avenue, San Francisco, CA 94133.

Federico García Lorca said that deep song floats like thistle-down in the wind. So too with stories. This novel is based on fact, held by memory, and woven in fantasy. Morón de la Frontera is a real place, one of the great, though little-known, music centers of the Western world. It was here in the 1960s and 1970s that I studied guitar and lived with my Gypsy friends. Diego del Gastor, Ansonini del Puerto, Fernanda de Utrero, and Joselero are the real names of masters of old-style flamenco. Paco de Lucía is a master of contemporary flamenco and world music. I have changed the names of other flamenco artists and friends, and as a writer of fiction I have invented freely.

D.R.

Striking those strings. Moving through chords.
There is nothing I love more!
Not eating. Not sleeping. Not sex.
A continuity of time in twelve beats.

I was not stolen by the Gypsies as a child.
I stole the Gypsies as my own.

Contents

Part One. *Soleares* / Song of Loneliness   1

Part Two. *Bulerías* / Song of Sensuality   57

Part Three. *Siguiriyas* / Song of Weeping   131

PART ONE

Soleares

Song of Loneliness

Chapter 1

This morning my song was strong, but the hands weak. The twelve beats were square and regal. The *compás*, the rhythmic frame, defined and solemn. And then I surprised myself with the memory of the old-style return. Instead of the expected three-beat refrain, I played that old dusty Morón style that Diego had taught. I can still see his hand as the thumb drove down on the A-string. His lips slightly pursed, the hollow of his cheeks deep and his eyes protruding.

Instead of playing the regulated six notes within the three beats, he played only three. As final and definitive as any three notes you could think of. A small form, if you will, of death. Silence followed in the next three beats, which most guitarists fill with sound. They don't think twice. Just fill it up. Here are three beats, make sounds with them. But you, Diego, what courage! To leave us alone for three beats. To leave us alone and to our own devices. Your music holds us in its arms, and we begin to enjoy dying.

What was it Mica said of Diego the first night I met her? "If Diego had only gone to bed that night. If he hadn't stayed up till dawn, he would have lived another decade." But he was never known to turn down a moment when the music might erupt. Only the afternoon can silence flamenco. That long stretch of hot sun.

The morning Diego died, the bells of the church rang the twelve beats of the *soleares* over and over. And we Americans living there wept for the father we had never had.

We foreigners had become the wanderers, returning home through the music. Season after season, year after year, we came for music lessons from all corners of the earth. Always traveling, we had changed places with the Gypsies.

Morón had labored for hundreds of years to produce one Diego del Gastor. Now he and his large Gypsy family were part of the stones the town was built on. Diego himself roamed only as far as the small Gypsy pueblos of Andalusia.

In those years, we would fly in and out of Madrid, train back and forth to Sevilla, and bus in and out of Morón. Diego's thumb anchored our shifting existence. We were seeking a home in an unbroken world, one in which Diego's generation was still firmly rooted. Once we began the study of the *falsetas,* the Andalusian air became a necessity. We became part of a extended international family that came together for the ritual festivals, fairs and lessons.

We found ourselves staying up all night in smoky bars to pick up a single *falseta,* or a new *picado* technique already rumored half way around the world to be faster than the old. We watched wooden virgins being carried out of churches in the middle of the night during Holy Week. Once I saw a black madonna lying abandoned next to a small bar; her carriers had begun their fiesta without her. We went to seasonal festivals, big and small. Gazpacho Festival in Morón in the summer. Harvest Festival in the fall. On the third day of the Feria of Sevilla, at three in the morning, I lay on a street ready to die from eating too many *churros* and drinking too much cognac. I considered this part of my study, part of what it took to earn the *falsetas*.

Falseta. I came to understand its meaning slowly as each one was etched in the memory of my hands. An original melodic phrase housed within the traditional unchanging rhythmic *compás*, a *falseta* passes through generations of Gypsy families. Each generation adds a new variation and becomes known for the history of its *falsetas*. In this way, a continuity between the living and the dead is always maintained.

My hands have forgotten many things. But this morning, though they were weak on the strings, they were strong in song.

Diego's *falseta* came to me, its electric presence suddenly making the index finger of my right hand twitch. Yes, it was from that dusty bag of Diego's tricks, and I knew it was coming even before it arrived.

The *compás* was driving strong. I was repeating, like some forsaken mantra, a *falseta* that was within my reach. Over and over I played that *falseta* and its answering *compás* until I created a cradle rocking.

It was then that my forgotten *falseta* friend appeared, as crystalline a counterpoint as you have ever heard. Within twelve beats an eternity of steps unwound. A long-legged spider with delicate glass legs danced up and down the steps. First one way. Then the next. Again back home, home to the ancient three-beat return. I noticed that my fingers ached. I cursed their weakness. They were never strong enough to channel those *falsetas*. "Tu tienes fuerza en el compás," the old ones said. You have power in the *compás*. "Pero, ella no tiene técnica," they said behind my back. They said this with no blame. How could I have technique when I had begun so late in life? My first sixteen years passed by without my playing a note. Wasted.

I was sixteen the summer my brother Aaron's hair grew below his ears, almost touching the collar of his Oxford blue shirt. Our parents disapproved. That extra two inches became a source of tense excitement for me. Watching his hair grow. Would it actually grow over his collar after he arrived in Berkeley or during our last summer home together?

Waiting for him to leave, I practiced nightly in my bedroom. Windows opened wide. Crickets pulsing. The fat leaves of summer pressed against the screens. In pink shorty pajamas, legs folded under me, hunched over the guitar, I played my few melodies. On my guitar case I had written a large sign, "I am not a folk singer." I had already learned three *soleá falsetas*. Puberty had begun for me as a quest for music. When I looked up, I could see myself in the mirror across from the bed. This is how I spent that last summer.

When the napkin arrived from the Bar Pepe, innocently enough, at our house on Sunnyridge Road I was not surprised.

Ordinary envelope. Foreign stamp. I never doubted that it would come. I had secretly written to the author of a book about the gypsies I had discovered in my guitar teacher's studio.

I snatched the letter from the foyer table and opened the envelope. Inside was a thin triangular napkin with a hand-drawn map in blue ink. Bus station: Sevilla. Pueblo: Morón. A crooked winding road connected these two points. A small childlike drawing of a bus traveled the line. "Ven, si tu quieres." Come if you wish, is all it said.

The sound of cicadas sawing the hot air began to penetrate my concentration. I looked out the open front door. I could see sprinklers making rainbows on the bathing suits of skinny children leaping through them. I knew the grass felt cool between their bare toes. A normal summer afternoon in the suburbs. I looked down again at the map. Everything had changed. My departure began here.

That night Aaron stood in the doorway watching me practice. Crossing over to the bed, he sat down behind me, my brush in his hand. I looked at the mirror and I watched him as he brushed my long black hair. We looked at each other in the mirror. There was still a little bit of time before he left for college. We could still change our names and move to California together. We'd had this idea for many years and we said it out loud for the last time. In between these brushings we had violent arguments or maintained a controlled indifference. It was not frustrated sex that drove us. It was frustrated tenderness.

We did not change our names. We didn't know then that what drove us to opposite ends of the world was the passionate closeness that kept us bound together. Aaron left for the West Coast. I left for Andalusia. It seemed Aaron was going forward in time and I was going back. The rim of the Pacific. The dust of Morón.

When I first entered Morón de la Frontera, it was like walking back into a dream that felt more real than waking life. It was a dream of a past that I had no knowledge of, but I immediately recognized it as the missing dimension. It was a more remote past than Eastern Europe, which was too soaked in the blood of my people to walk again in this lifetime. But Morón with its charming vital small town life, Morón with its heritage of art, Morón with its castle crumbling on the hill; Morón would do just fine.

By the time I arrived, Diego wasn't teaching women the guitar. Here's why. Years before, one of Diego's students, named Sondra, fell in love with him, so the story goes. Diego, and this had been much-discussed, was celibate. That was a fact, but the reasons for his celibacy were disputed. Was it sainthood or impotency? Did his total involvement in his art drain his sexuality, or was all his sexuality pouring into his art giving it more depth? These two themes were often argued back and forth among the foreigners in Bar Pepe. The various Gypsies were strangely mute on this topic.

In any case, Sondra was in love, and Diego stopped giving her lessons. This was devastating to Sondra, who began a daily vigil in Bar Pepe, drinking one glass of wine after another as each day moved into evening. Her only focus was Diego. And then it happened. One day, she pulled a small revolver out of her garter belt and shot at him. So goes the story. Diego escaped unharmed out of Bar Pepe's infamous back door. He swore on the grave of his mother never to give classes to women again. Sondra continued to watch him.

My first years in Morón she could be seen every day, in the corner. She was distinguished-looking. She spoke to no one, except Pepe, the owner and bartender of the Bar Pepe. Pepe had taken to supplying her with free drinks years before. They called her La Loca Perdida, the Crazy Lost One. Morón took care of its crazy people. In Morón there was no such thing as flight. All things returned to Bar Pepe.

Whatever passed between friends during the day, or between lovers during the night, was known, mysteriously, the next day by Pepe. And more likely than not the very person that one wanted to avoid at all costs was there, across the not-so-crowded bar. And so, for this reason, one conversation could span a lifetime and often did. So too with the *falseta*. One musical idea was repeated relentlessly as the clear fall days passed into the chilling, wet winters. And this idea, this *falseta*, as the winter days grew darker, would be embellished the way the telling of a single tale could grow during a long winter evening. Then, with the coming of summer, that *falseta*, having gained stature through its lasting power, would enter the whole body of the form. Years later, when hearing some *falseta*, I was likely to have images of the particular winter in which it developed. An image of Sondra for example, standing in the corner of the bar, wearing a neat skirt and sweater, her hair freshly done at the beauty parlor, and her vacant, haunted eyes as she followed Diego's every move.

Her effect on my education was that I never studied with Diego directly. And so his youngest nephew, Manuel, became my first teacher instead. Perhaps this was for the better. Nonetheless, Diego was very fond of me. He insisted on taking me to all the fiestas, where I sat on his left side. In between songs he would often stroke my cheek. These men who are mothers!

One could not hear Diego play and remain unchanged. In the silence between the notes, it was possible to hear the crickets even when there were none, and to feel the spray of a waterfall in the falling notes of a *soleá falseta*. When the sound of the guitar stopped there was a resonance in the bar for hours afterward. One could see it glowing in the faces of those who had heard. And so the experience was not just hearing this music, but being with others who were opened for that moment in the same way.

One day, early in my first stay in Morón, I got up the nerve to ask Diego, despite what I knew, to teach me the *siguiriyas*, the song of weeping, the song of death. It seemed to me not too difficult, as its rhythmic frame, its *compás*, rocked between six beats, instead of twelve. The night before I had heard an old man sing it, accompanied by Diego. It felt familiar to me, the old voice wailing like the shofar horn blowing on Yom Kippur. I didn't know then that this form was as serious as the blowing of the horn on the high holiday. I just knew that within the sound I felt suddenly at home.

I was not prepared for Diego's response. He was sitting in Bar Pepe at the time playing dominos in the afternoon light, with two other older gentlemen. I had interrupted their game to pose this request.

"Teach me," I said. "Teach me the *siguiriyas*."

First Diego looked at me for a long time. Then he smiled, and began to laugh. He turned to the other men and repeated my question several times. Three to be exact. For some unknown reason, most Gypsies in Morón repeated all thoughts three times just as they did with *falsetas*. Finally he pulled me close to him and said, "Child. Do you think you could learn a thing like this at your age? What are they teaching the young children in America? What could you possibly know of this mood? No. Absolutely not. You tell Manuel to teach you alegrías." And with this he shooed me out of the bar.

"¡Qué alegría!" is a favorite phrase to describe an outburst of joy. And *alegrías* is the form for happiness. All forms fall into two dimensions: the light and the deep. Alegrías was considered to be *cante chico*, the light song. And I wanted only to do with *cante jondo*, the deep song.

By the time I reached Manuel that evening, he and everyone else had heard the story. In fact, Diego never tired of repeating it to whomever would listen. It seemed to give him some special insight into Los Estados Unidos.

Alegrías is kids' stuff, I thought to myself as I suddenly found myself standing outside the bar door, the afternoon sun glaring in my eyes. "And I won't learn it!" I declared out loud.

It wasn't easy talking Manuel into a compromise. "What do I know about happiness?" I told his bemused face over and over. "At least let me learn *soleares*, the song of loneliness," I argued. About being alone, I knew enough to last most Gypsies a lifetime. Manuel agreed, not out of understanding, but out of respect for my intensity. Intensity was a quality that the Gypsies equate with seriousness.

Soleares was thought of as the mother of all the forms. *Soleares* — to be alone. Morón was the region famous for this form. An ironic development, for "being alone" was frowned upon, and seemed to me to almost never occur in this town. Solitariness was viewed as an illness, something to be remedied immediately. And yet the loneliness of the *soleá cante* was nowhere more deeply expressed.

Twenty years later in a studio in Sevilla, I finally understood the *alegrías*. A five-year-old was dancing it and had captivated those of us watching, when suddenly I recalled a special *falseta* Diego used to play. And this *letra*:

> Todos le llevan al niño
> Yo no tengo que llevarle
> Le llevaré una camisa
> Que se la ponga su madre

> Everyone takes presents to the baby
> I have nothing to take
> So I'll take a little shirt
> For his mother to put on him.

It was then I knew that *alegrías* can be heard for what it is only by young people with old souls or old people with the souls of children. A genetic Gypsy characteristic. At sixteen,

I was neither young enough nor old enough to hear it for what it was. Perhaps I had no alternative but to learn the *soleá*. And so for the next decade I played only *soleares*. The song of loneliness. Its *compás*. Its *falsetas*. And its chords which called forth the deep song.

Chapter 2

Before you died, I traveled light. "Happy is the land that has no history," I was fond of saying. Let's pretend this is home.

My suitcase for Spain is packed with mementos. Small relics that you'd think were not necessary. The common advice is "travel light" and take only those fabrics that do not wrinkle when washed. A folding iron for the one good dress. A small pad for notes. Three skirts. No shorts in Spain. Some cotton T-shirts and of course a sturdy pair of walking shoes.

But I ignore these words. It is a form of arrogance in part, but also I am driven. My suitcase is overflowing and I begin to section off, one at a time, small corners of my house. Here and there, piles of words like leaves — wet, of different colors, on the hard autumn ground. And now the suitcase overflows with wet-leaved words. Words such as "forsaking all others." Words such as "the air was soft but also sadness was felt."

Tonight, the moon is full and bores a silver, dusty path, a dusty, silver hole, a third eye in my head. I suddenly wake and feel I must see if I can close the suitcase. I sit hard on the old leather. The suitcase rocks as I lean from one side to the other, and memories seep out through the cracks.

I discard the fold-up iron, despite my mother's warning about the possibility of wrinkles. I throw clothes out over my head, now kneeling in front of the open suitcase, frantically rearranging to make room. Just what am I making room for? Oh no, not that. It is the nightmare I thought I was rid of. Perhaps if I remove it, there will be room after all for that cotton T-shirt I am so fond of.

I light a cigarette and rock back on my knees. I remember the night I first dreamed you were dead, Aaron, buried, under my bed. When I tried to pull you out I saw you as a small boy of eight, my older brother, sitting on the side of the summer swimming pool. Your lips were blue, as they were prone to be, and your teeth chattered but you smiled at the same time. I wanted to shield you from the cold, but you kept on shivering. Your thin but sturdy body. I love you still.

But this was years ago, and now I have a wild thought. I'll put one of your old sweaters in the suitcase. You were known to wear especially warm sweaters. Even in Los Angeles you had this tendency to shiver. Here's the rust-colored one I took from your apartment. Sometimes I would put it on. Your smell was still on it. Mother insisted I have it cleaned, but I defied her. Your smell, musky and sleeplike. I put that sweater in the bottom of the suitcase and lay the white T-shirt carefully over it. The cool whiteness of cotton over the musky wool.

I have decided, at least almost for sure, to put your pain

in too. I know that it might involve another suitcase, perhaps a duffle bag. For now I'll just place it in the corner with the pile of "almost sure things" until Mica comes by.

My friend Mica, midwife to my journeys, always helps me pack. The night before leaving, she comes over and does a sorting. She knows well the dangerous loss of definition that one can incur when traveling. The air inside my apartment has already grown thin with my departure.

Mica's foray into the flamenco world began even earlier than mine did. It began in the womb. When her father, Cesar, was a small child, his father took him to Sevilla many times. It was their long, six-month boat trips that attuned Cesar's mind to a different sense of time. Once when a drunk taxi driver careening through the narrow alleyways of Sevilla invited Cesar to Morón, because he longed to hear Diego play a *soleares* then and there, Cesar accepted. They reached Morón de la Frontera that early dawn in time to hear a seasoned *soleares* straight from Diego's thumb. It was the power of that very thumb that pulled Mica into her own yearly journeys to this preindustrial world of ranting fiestas. I understood. I, too, was swept into Diego's orbit for half a lifetime.

The last time Mica helped me pack I was going back to Andalusia as I had for many springs. In a last-minute tribute to whimsy, we had put in the red silk dress. "In honor of La Feria de Sevilla," Mica had pronounced as we finished the ritual bottle of wine.

I returned from that trip with the caked mud of Feria still on my ankles and a wilted flower pinned to my long black hair. It had rained solid during the whole week of Feria, the dirt paths outside the tents turning to rivers of mud, traversed by the Spanish girls wearing needle-thin high-heeled shoes.

The morning I left, straight from the *caseta*, the tent where Manuel was still playing as the sun was just beginning to rise, there was a pair of those shoes, abandoned in the mud in the middle of the main street of that makeshift *feria* city on the outskirts of Sevilla. The fires of the old Gypsy women were burning low, and the wet and tired Gypsy children huddled close in. The women gestured to me, a solitary figure, wet and wilted from the rain, tears making tracks of lightness against the dust on my face. They gestured with that Spanish wave that means "goodbye" in America, but "come here" in Spain. "¡Niña, niña! ¿Porque estás llorando? La lluvia es bastante, no niña?" Child, why are you crying? Isn't the rain enough?

Now my hair is short, styled after the fashion of the day. And what will Mica say to this extra bag?

Aaron. The wall between our bedrooms was so thin. I could always hear you moaning on Sunday nights. Sunday meant that the next day was Monday, and that meant school. Your desperate attempt to avoid this dreaded encounter with the outside world was to push your dresser against the door. A barricade of sorts. We all had to push hard against it — Mother, Father, and I — to let the doctor in to deliver a soothing shot of Demerol. You usually slept it off all the next day and the car pool went along without you. The doctor always said, "There appears to be a knot in his stomach." All the appropriate tests were negative, but the knots kept appearing.

On the other side of the wall, I developed a small "Sunday night knot" in response, though they had forbidden me to go into your room, climb into your bed, and hold you until your breathing returned to normal. I remember your slight young snore on the inhale, almost a breeze it was. For many Monday mornings they had found me there, my eyes wide open and yours closed and peaceful.

"It's not good for her to be in bed with him like this," the doctor had said in all seriousness to our parents. "And he must learn not to gain attention after this fashion. If he doesn't learn now, he never will."

And so we all lay there listening. The parents on their side of the wall, and I on mine. Listening to your moan. Listening until I thought I would bang my head right through that wall. But then I would hear Mother's voice saying, "Mort, we must call the doctor. Mort, he's in pain. Whatever the reason, for God's sake call Dr. Zimmerman."

And then the muted doorbell downstairs and the slow steps through the hall. The black bag making its way up the steps.

I've made up my mind for sure. Your pain comes or I'm not going. There's no wall between us now and I'll take with me what I want.

Through an accident of fate, I discovered the sound of the flamenco guitar. By discovery I mean that the wood of the guitar smelled like ancient forests. I detected a small wind against my face when opening the guitar case. This wind had crossed a cemetery of years. I also noted a fine red dust that covered the chamois cloth protecting the top of the instrument. It was a great gift that my first teacher, a simple man, had experienced that same wind, seen that red dust. And this is why the music entered me the way that it did.

By the end of a year I had surpassed my first teacher. He gave me his guitar, and with that giving, he gave me the wind. My second teacher, de la Mata, was an elderly gentleman from Madrid who had left Spain when Franco took over, and brought me closer to its essence. It was something about the way he assumed that he, a sixty-year-old man, would have something of value to give to a fourteen-year-old girl. De la Mata played classical flamenco. Trained at the conservatory in Madrid, he had devised a complex system of notation to pin down this elusive art. It was in his library, while waiting for a lesson, that I found the book with a picture in it of an old Gypsy man playing the guitar. The caption read: "For us, the deep song, like our tears, will always be a part of our life." I thought I saw evidence of the fine red dust in the lines of the old Gypsy's face.

By the time de la Mata found me, it was too late. It was as if some part of my soul that had previously had no form, and yet was the source of my urgency, had found a home. His protestations concerning the Gypsies' evil ways did nothing but confirm my conviction that these were the chosen people, the ones who knew the language of my spirit.

But at this point another story always intrudes, one that is not so romantic. It is, of course, a story about grief. Perhaps it could start like this: as we grow older our griefs, like our bodies, become our constant companions. See the coast in the morning grey light! How it seems to be a story that goes on with no end.

"He's gone, Loren," my father said to me, "We've lost him."

I knew. I knew as I drove up to the house. I knew it was Aaron. When the phone rang, I thought, "Don't answer that phone." It rang and it rang until I picked it up and threw it across the room and then it rang again. I was numb.

"He's gone. He was supposed to show up at Bernie's for dinner and when he didn't come, . . ." I listened to my father's voice.

"What do you mean, he was supposed to go to Bernie's?" I asked, as if that mattered.

"Bernie called, and he said to me, 'Mort, he's gone.' "

My mother had said: "Don't answer the phone, Mort. Please."

My mother's mother had dreamt that night that someone just out of reach was sobbing. All night the crying continued. She woke to find her daughter by her side. My mother. My grandmother's dream pursued itself until dawn.

I kept taking showers. I sat naked on the bathroom floor as the water poured over me. I saw ducks bathing in the dawn light, their green-black feathers turning faintly orange. They have no dreams, I thought. And we, so slow, labor toward waking.

My brother is dead. He's still dead. He was dead last night. He is continuing to be dead. Ha! I've figured it out.

Aaron's still dead. It's the next day. A friend drives me to meet my parents, who have flown out from New York.

I hold the body that once held mine. It is my mother. She comes off the plane first, escorted by a stewardess. My mother is being held up, and they are transfering this holding to me. It seems that these stewardesses know. What do they know?

A mother lost a son. There's Mort. Insistence in his gait. His posture. I'll take charge here. Of what? Aaron's gone. Mort is greeting his father. He's under control. Fierce control. But where is Mort? I don't see him. I see control. Control, for his father. But it's all out now, Mort. There's no more hiding. Ha! The pain is out. Don't laugh. Holding down hysterics.

Hug your grandmother. Her face. She crossed the ocean, crossed a century, from a shtetl. Tragedy is a part of her life. But not this kind. No, your grandson was not killed by a Cossack. What then? What is the story here?

Mort and my grandfather discuss plans. Plans for the funeral, plans for the eulogy. Wait just a moment here. We have not gone ten steps and they are discussing plans. Can you go ten steps without fear?

Last night when I looked at the moon, it was a crushed hat, discarded, on the hill. The magnolia tree had blossomed before the leaves.

The waves pulled back over the small pebbles every night. Over and over the sound of small pebbles tumbling backward into the sea. Strange how we start with death and move backward into life.

The night after Aaron died, his friends met in a large house in the Hollywood Hills to hold a memorial service. Their big dispute evidently was not whether to have drugs at the gathering but whether to have nitrous oxide. Imagine. They had to reconstruct his face for the open casket. It was purple and green from the nitrous. Puffy. Bernie said when they found him he was still warm. The skin still warm, but the face purple.

Mother had already moved into the isolation she would inhabit for the next seven years. She never wanted to see his friends again. She knew what had killed him. To her it was perfectly clear. The West Coast had killed him as sure as that gas had traveled through his veins. Everywhere she looked she saw the instruments of his death. And in these instruments she faced her dreams for him. She saw death in the cars speeding around the corners of Sunset Boulevard. She saw death in the marquees of the movie houses. In the backyard swimming pools. And worst of all, when she looked out at the Pacific, she saw how easily she had mistaken expanse for optimism.

Mort didn't go to the memorial. He was drinking Scotch and he was making phone calls one after another. That's what he knew how to do.

I went. But I went for all the wrong reasons. What could the right ones be? It had been ten years since our last shared summer. I went because I was fascinated with his world. I wanted to meet his friends. Finally I would discover what he had withheld from me. That part of him would be mine at last.

I was obsessed with what to wear. And walking through the alien streets of Beverly Hills, I was not alone in this obsession. I had never met his friends, but I had heard about each one for years. I wanted to look good. I wanted an image. I had no cover.

Click went the imagined camera as I walked the streets searching for an image to allow me into his world. I felt guilty that I wasn't thinking of Aaron. I didn't yet know that I was beginning the long and painful journey through my grief.

Click. I bought a suede coat for three hundred dollars. "Who bought this coat?" I wondered walking out of the store.

Click. I was lost to myself.

But when the door opened to the house in the hills, I had a cover. A breathtaking image, I thought. The suede coat, a flowered silk shirt, tight jeans and heels, scarf tied casually around my neck.

Elizabeth, a poised woman in her mid-forties, opened the door and embraced me. In the background, through the embrace, I saw a large group of people sitting around a glass table. There they were. All the characters in my — or was it my brother's? — drama. My heart began to race. The cozy-looking Berkeley friends; the weather-worn-looking Big Sur friends; the glamorous and famous L.A. friends. I was guided into the circle of light by the hand that opened the door. I was at the edge of the circle.

Inside the circle food was being eaten. Wine, white and chilled, was being served. Talk, clever and insightful, was being shared. I took a step down one of the two stairs into the living room. I took a step into the circle.

"This is Aaron's sister," is the last thing I remembered Elizabeth saying, as I fell down the steps onto the glass table, the brie and caviar flying.

Everyone moved to help at once. No one moved. Click.

A hand was there to lift me up, to lead me out of the living room into a quiet study. I was weeping. I couldn't catch my breath. I was sobbing. My grief had officially begun.

Chapter 3

Practicing scales on the guitar, or even thinking of practicing scales on my guitar, is a form of meditation that doesn't make the air too thin.

I can hear Doug say, "The fingers on the left hand form an arch across the neck. Four small, perfect arches moving up the neck."

I can hear Rafael say: "Más despacio, más despacio. . ." More slowly, more slowly. Play more slowly, so that when it counts, you can move more quickly.

And I hear my old teacher de la Mata in his broken English urging: "No tension in the hand, no tension in the heart," and then showing me how his hand hangs naturally across the strings, the snow falling outside the steamy windows of his studio, the wood of his guitar gleaming warm and bright.

After I first injured my right hand, I thought I'd have to give up these scale-practicing meditations. But I developed a way to continue even when I couldn't play. I just imagined the strings and the hand arching over them.

We all have a trail of broken guitars behind us. Everyone has a story about injuries to our right hands. Diego's story is more famous than mine. But to tell his, I must tell mine also, and this principle I have been faithful to throughout.

The unusual truth about Diego is that he never owned his own guitar. At least not for long. He would be drawn to someone else's guitar, and that someone most often would lend it over, so to speak. But one year the aficionados of Morón, rich and poor alike, decided that it was a disgrace that Diego del Gastor, the prize of Morón, did not have his own guitar.

A small benefit was drummed up. A benefit for the guitar of Diego. A committee, the likes of which you would never see anywhere else, was formed to search for the perfect guitar. The committee was made up of the following characters: Ansonini, one of the grand *festeros* of all time. He knew nothing about guitars, but was crucial to the functioning of committee gatherings because of his love of cognac and his propensity to break into song. A truly great *festero* can stimulate a spontaneous fiesta at just the right moment. Ansonini was of this vintage. A successful garlic soup was quite enough to ignite a full-blown fiesta, and he knew this. Ansonini could measure group joy to such an accurate degree that he was never wrong. Not about the ingredients for a good soup or a good fiesta. Angelote the olive grower, the token non-Gypsy, and the money behind the project. Manuel, whose sweet nature was essential to keep small disagreements from overwhelming the goal. Enrique, a spiteful and mean Gypsy with a black humor, and one of the most profound voices for the deep song in Andalusia. And two or three local barroom regulars, just to add to the democratic process.

After months of meetings and small fiestas, the group decided that a Barba would be the appropriate jewel and the very afternoon of the decision they hired a taxi for Sevilla, and all piled in to go to speak to Francisco Barba in person. I would have given my right arm, to say nothing of my hand, to have been in that taxi! To have spent the afternoon with them in Barba's shop discussing a matter of such importance, and to have gone along with them later in the evening as they celebrated their wisdom in the bars of Triana, the oldest Gypsy neighborhood in Sevilla.

I can only say that I was there the night the guitar was presented to Diego. I saw his face, awestruck both by the quality of the guitar and by the exquisite fact that everyone had kept a secret from him for so long. The fiesta that ensued is still being talked about twenty years later, and the grand finale, when Diego, totally drunk, sat on the guitar, breaking it beyond repair, is still being toasted.

I can assure you that my own story is less glamorous than that. But the story of my first injury has more importance here, and at least a slight flair of drama. It happened my first summer in Morón, during my first lesson with Manuel, after Diego had proclaimed that he should teach me the *alegrías*. The initial meeting and the initial injury have always since been bound together.

When I say the phrase, "summer in Morón," I refer to an oven of air that reduces even the hardiest of souls. Life begins only after nine at night, and even then any slight breeze is appreciated. Above all, Morón is an inland habitation. There is nothing of the sea, or sea breezes, about Morón. That night there was no breeze and a fan was using up electricity in the small basement room under the *finca*, the ranch house where I was staying.

I was nervously waiting for Manuel, practicing scales. I was drinking cheap wine when he entered the room. He said, "Hola," and reached out his hand to shake mine. His smile, then so sweet, caused my heart to race. With my other hand, I reached over to the fan to turn it toward him, a gesture of goodwill and more than that, an attempt to cool the heat that was rising between us. I reached into its turning blades. There was so much blood flying that it was difficult at first to see how badly I was hurt. Manuel fainted and that was that. I ran out of the room yelling in English for a doctor. A ranch hand who spoke English wrapped a clean rag around the single injured finger, and we left immediately in his Land Rover for town, leaving Manuel on the floor to regain consciousness.

We never found a doctor, but at a *farmacia* we roused the pharmacist and he bandaged the tip of the middle finger tightly to hold it together. That was my first and last lesson that summer. I prayed that I would play again. My hand stayed bandaged, and to this day when held straight out, the tip of my middle finger is curved and nonresponsive to delicate messages from the brain. By this I mean that it cannot accomplish a *trémolo*. Fortunately this is of minor import in the "pure" art. In fact, the *trémolo* is considered by some to be "non-Gypsy," a phrase you do not want applied to your playing.

There is one *trémolo* passage in Diego's *soleares*, however, that turns the heart, and to say I have no regret about my finger that cannot play it would not be the truth. But it was from this wound that I first learned to "imagine the strings," and this has proved invaluable. More than once it has been crucial to my survival. And this, too, I came to know from that summer: You can't learn this skill by imagining an injury. The wound must be real, and only from that point can the rest be imagined.

Chapter 4

Only in Spain is a dead man more alive than the living. In Morón one has to pay rent on the bones of one's ancestors. The cemetery on the outskirts of town does not grow larger as the generations turn. Just deeper. Each family buys its plot, yes. But the plot is no bigger than one grave wide. It is deep, though. Like an upside-down skyscraper, the bodies buried one on top of the other. And the bodies only two feet under still send up a stench into the glittering blue air of summer. In the corner of the cemetery is a fenced-in area filled with scorched white bones. These are the homeless bones. One can only guess at their stories. Perhaps during a hard, cold, wet winter it had come down to feeding the children or housing the bones. Not as easy a decision as you would imagine. The role of the sun in the quick and efficient scorching of rotting flesh is never taken for granted in Morón. The bones gleam silver at night like large utensils.

It was time to remove Tuerto's bones from his coffin and place them in a small burial box now that the necessary seven years had passed. This ritual is what you might call rent control for the dead. Only families that made no money could apply for this benefit. The Gypsies of Morón qualified. They never made money. They made songs. Rafael, Tuerto's nephew, to this day contends that the seven-year regulation has nothing to do with bureaucracy. He says the seven years is a sacred ritual. It is done so you'll know, once and for all, that your relative, your mother, your brother, your loved one, is dead.

Regardless of the inspiration of the regulation, in July of 1956, Tuerto's seven years were up and not one of his family, which numbered one hundred strong, volunteered to move his bones. They were all more than willing to give a fiesta in exchange for his rent. They couldn't be faulted for lack of generosity on his behalf. That is, now that he was dead. It was fear that kept them from standing up for the task. They had feared him when he was alive and seven years had not made a dent in their feelings. And so they feared him when he was dead, in all the same ways. The only shift was that the fear had grown now that he was no longer in sight, skulking about the streets or lying in the gutters drunk. Now that he was dead, he lived in their imaginations.

Some family history. There were three sons in the large extended family. Bernardo, Diego's younger brother, lost his mind before he had one; but he was loved. The fact that he would sometimes leave a pile of shit on the church's altar for the Sunday congregation did not dampen the family's affections. Tuerto, Diego's older brother, was the family drunk and he was hated and shunned by all. Whether Diego himself set the tone for this hatred no one knew for sure. In all other ways, from the long shock of white hair that fell across his otherwise bald head, to his cherished *alegrías falsetas*, Diego was a saint. But where Tuerto was involved, the devil in Diego came to the fore. No one was the least bit disillusioned with Diego because of this seeming paradox. They had heard him play his *siguiriyas* and had felt the dark side of Diego's moon.

The brothers had two sisters, each of whom produced two sons. Manuel and Ángel are brothers. Jesús and Rafael are brothers. Manuel and Rafael were suckled on the same teat. How do I know? I was told by a reliable source, the mother. They were suckled by Jesús's and Rafael's mother, Diego's sister, because hers was the only available teat. So Manuel, Ángel, Rafael, and Jesús are all Diego's nephews, and together they make up a genius equal to that of their uncle on the flamenco guitar. None, individually, however, is anywhere near his equal, a phenomenon discussed for over thirty years in the Bar Pepe. The nephews are followed with scrutiny by the large Gypsy family, all of whom hope the miracle of Diego's *toque* — his lifework — will be repeated.

It might be too simple to say that the source of Diego's hatred was Tuerto's creation of a *soleá falseta* that was rumored to be *más jondo* and *más gitano* than any one of the hundreds of *falsetas* in Diego's *toque* of *soleá*. If the whole of Diego's *toque* was likened to a cathedral, which it often was, then his *soleá falsetas* were the stained-glass windows of the deepest and warmest hues — the glaring light of the white afternoon streaming through them, deep purple, blue, and red.

In comparison Tuerto's *toque* was a hut. Like the old, crumbling, adobe hut he lived in on the outskirts of town. The white walls were streaked with dry mud and the scorpions crawled slowly sideways across the dirt floor. The fingernails of the left hand normally kept cropped by any serious guitarist who had in mind to press down the strings between the frets were in Tuerto's case as long as a spider's thin legs. The nails on his right hand were cracked beyond repair except the thumbnail, which was in surprisingly perfect form and condition.

His technique as a result consisted almost entirely of the *pulgar*, the thumb and, though limited, this is what gave his playing the "pure" sound sought by all. Even a bar full of arguing Gypsies would agree that the *pulgar* is the key to the deep sound, the *jondo* style. It was said that a non-Gypsy had no thumb.

Tuerto had no *trémolo,* no *rasgueado,* and no *picado* in his technique. He was all thumb. And because of the length of his left-hand fingernails, the notes he played were what you would call "dirty." That is, the notes did not ring clear. This "dirt" is yet another elusive quality necessary for the flamenco guitar. That deep song always needs a certain amount of dirt is unanimously acknowledged. But how much dirt can a song take and still be a song? This issue of degree would never be agreed on by any two Gypsies.

Tuerto's *soleá* was all dirt and all thumb. And though he was not sober one day in his long life, his *falsetas* rang dry as the scorched summer bones in the fenced-in corral of the Morón cemetery. He preferred to play only *soleá*, the song of loneliness. Even at that he invented only a limited number of *falsetas*. It was said also that on one good day he created three exquisite *falsetas* of *alegría*, although some claimed that Diego early on, perhaps as early as adolescence, stole these three, though I myself cannot believe this. What would Diego need with these three *falsetas* of Tuerto's, especially from the song of happiness? Tuerto, as far as I know, had had only one joyful day in his life.

But Tuerto, when lying in the gutter, would rant about the stolen three. He would curse Diego to any passerby that would lend an ear. "¡Me cago en sus muertos!" I shit on his dead, he'd howl. This curse always came back to haunt him, for Diego and he shared the same dead. He became increasingly protective of his *soleá* and as a result never played at a bar or at a fiesta. By the time he was twenty-one he was a recluse.

He was shunned by Diego and the whole family, supposedly because he was an alcoholic, though every one of them started each day off with a shot of gin at Bar Pepe. Ansonini went so far as to brush his teeth, all three of them, with gin, as some kind of statement.

The four nephews, however, Jesús, Ángel, Manuel and Rafael, all secretly took lessons from Tuerto. Had this been found out, Diego would have shut the door tight to his own cathedral. It was the only secret, the only bond among the four that transcended family feuds, daily *guasa,* and the love of the same woman or any woman.

Tuerto taught each one equally, two different *falsetas* of his *soleá*. He forbade them to ever play these *falsetas* to each other or in public as long as he lived. There were ten *falsetas* all told. Among the four nephews eight were accounted for. The four nephews search the globe for the missing two. They fear that Tuerto out of spite gave them to a foreign student of flamenco. Perhaps one that bought him drinks and sat next to him, with his rank breath and rotting teeth.

Now, the deadline for the transfer of bones from coffin to box was July 15th. The night before, a wild fiesta at the bar had ensued. The only form played was the *siguiriya*, the song of weeping, or the song of death. The literal translation of *siguiriya* is "one day follows the next." That it was played all night was highly unusual, as most fiestas begin with the *cante chico*, the light song, an *alegrías* for example. Or at the very least a *bulerías*, the song of sensuality, and a transition into the deep song. It is only toward dawn, after hours of *soleares*, that the *siguiriya* is drawn out. Only toward dawn when light can almost be seen breaking like a wave on the horizon. But that night they began *siguiriya* in the afternoon and by ten o'clock it seemed that dawn would never break. The father of Jesús, sang an ancient and beloved *letra* of the *siguiriya* over and over:

Rompe la oscuridad de la noche
Pero en realidad es nuestra pena
Rompiéndose dentro de nosotros

They say each morning the dawn breaks
But really it is our own grief
Breaking within us...

The cognac was like blood and tears, flowing freely. It seemed, after all, that they had never grieved Tuerto.

At last when the real dawn broke, Rafael came forth. He stood on his chair and announced, cross-eyed with drink and sorrow, that he would walk the road to the cemetery and there deliver Tuerto's bones from coffin to box. Mateo, the man with two rows of teeth and a close friend of Rafael's, surprised everyone by offering to join Rafael. He was inspired. Rafael was drunk.

From the castle crumbling on the hill one can get an overview of the town. Had we been sitting there that morning we would have seen two small figures staggering arm in arm down the road to the left of town over the hill, across the small river and through the gate of the cemetery.

The wind usually blew from one direction, from the west. Because the town is due west of the cemetery, the smell of death almost never infiltrated daily life. The cry of death often came through the deep song, but the smell of death was something else altogether.

When the wind blew west, the *duendes,* the ghosts, were afoot. And though the smell was dreaded, the deep song that brought with it the *duendes* was valued above all, above life itself. When the cry of the song connected with the west wind, *duende* was brought into the room. It was then that the familiar was sent away and the tracks of the dead stretched out before each person's eyes.

Whether the purity of the cry of the artists' *soleares* or *siguiriya* changed the direction of the wind, or the wind wrenched the cry out of the artists' souls was not known. What was known for sure was that when the *duende* came there was a radical change of form, and all of them, deep within their music, were somehow changed from the inside out.

Duende could come in a small movement of the dancer's hand. In the beginning *"ahí"* of the singer's chant. In the dirt of the thumb as the guitarist's hand closed in on a D-minor chord. Or in sudden tears, a heartfelt *"olé,"* or curse of a listener lost in the moment. When it came, it came suddenly and without mercy. All were reduced by it, all longed for it.

The morning of July 15th, as you might already have guessed, the wind blew from the west. By the time poor Rafael and Mateo passed through the gate, they were sober but sick with the smell. They pushed against the stench as some hikers close to the top of a mountain will lean into the wind in order to persevere. When they arrived at the grave site good fortune was with them and the wind stilled.

Both testify to the fact that when they opened the grave, Tuerto lay peaceful and intact, staring up at them. Though they only viewed him for an instant, they are as sure of that as the day is long. And then the wind picked up, and the next moment they were staring down at his bones.

The people of the town who believe this vision explain it by saying that the alcohol in Tuerto's blood preserved an illusion of him. A kind of pickled effect. Those who don't believe any of it credit the "fiesta of the *siguiriya*" as the cause of the hallucination.

However, one unexplained fact remains. Rafael, before the wind came up — driven by a force that was not his, since he is not brave — reached down and grabbed Tuerto's thumbnail. For many years, he wore it around his neck. Rafael now knows three of Tuerto's *falsetas*.

Chapter 5

Before my first lesson with Rafael, on one of my visits to Morón, I asked Mica to write a note on my hand in Spanish so I wouldn't forget. The note said:

Mis manos tiemblan. Pero tengo razón.
Y no tengo miedo.

An adequate translation would be, "My hands tremble. But I am not afraid. I have my reasons." This was a lie. I was afraid. But it was also the truth that my hands had trembled from birth. I was three months premature, and so spent those early months in a shoebox, where the tremor started. When I finally arrived home, Aaron is reported to have said, "Take her back. She is three months too late."

But I wasn't going to explain all that to Rafael. My Spanish wasn't good enough and at that point I didn't know he would understand. Later that evening, after I told him, he claimed to have been in that shoebox with me. He is prone to exaggeration because of his extreme generosity of spirit, but nonetheless, he wants our bones, mine and his, buried together. Knowing Rafael was the closest I ever came to a teat. In his family, there always seemed to be room for one more person.

When I arrived at his house, I said to him, "I want to play with my back to you." He sat me down behind the couch with a bottle of cognac and said that essential words. "¡T-o-c-a!" Play!

I played *soleares*. The one that Manuel had taught me when I first came to Móron at sixteen. I played the *soleares* that I had been practicing for ten years. Diego had taught Manuel, and Manuel had taught me, to play the silence between the notes like a bell. And the last *falseta* I played was the secret *falseta* of Tuerto's bones, the one that had the dryness of sound I had first heard ringing in the valley between the mountains outside of Morón.

Rafael wept. He came to me and cradled my head in both his hands. "Cara almeja," he crooned, "una almeja con ojos borrachos."

"Rafael," I said, "Rafael, why do you call me like a lover, call me 'drunk clam eyes'?"

"You play *soleares* like Diego when Diego was too drunk to play. And you have stolen a Tuerto *falseta!*" he said with admiration, his eyes slightly closed and with a touch of envy. Some people, whose motivations I do not trust, have said of me that I used these men to gain entrance to the cathedral of *falsetas*, of which Diego, the uncle, is the Holy Ghost. This is not true. They are jealous. And Rafael knew this.

It was then that he offered to teach me *bulerías*, the mocking, flirtatious form. I caught my breath. That pulsing rhythm. That driving *compás*. Those twelve beats that varied slightly, turned the loneliness of the *soleares* into the demonic sensuality of *bulerías*.

"¡Tu! Tu no tienes cojones. No puedes tocar por bulerías. Eso es," the old ones once told me when I asked to be taught the *bulerías*. You! You have no balls. You cannot learn the *bulerías*.

Rafael however refused to begin my *bulerías* education without first knowing how I had learned the secret *falseta* of Tuerto. It was a long story, but the night was young and the bottle of cognac full. I told it as I'll tell you. It was roundabout, but Rafael had said, "Dime la verdad." Tell me the truth. And that is what I gave him. *La verdad.*

The morning Leslie and I walked the dirt road outside of Morón, the town faded, and with it the night's humiliation. As we moved into the valley, the clanging of goat bells — some near, some distant — began like a soft rain of grief, lightning bugs of sound. Now close, now far. The ridge on our left was a soft mauve color and the stars hanging still, dim but present, were faded pearls in the early morning. In front of us, the moon, and on the right, the sun beginning, burning red and intimate. Clang . . . clang . . . clang . . . clang. . . . The deep clanging of the bells and the town fading like last night's dreams. The road before us was solitary and blue.

In town, Leslie had said, "Those bastards!" and he had meant it. There he had seemed brave. But now as we walked the five miles to the hut, he was shy and unsure of himself. Purple blemishes appeared beneath his light morning stubble. His hand in mine was muggy, thin, and insectlike.

Leslie was blond and English, but that was not his fault. The foreign men seemed glaringly inadequate next to the young Gypsies. Just by smoking a cigarette, the Gypsies expressed a style, or more to the point, a form that told you they knew who they were. The kind of crisis that was so familiar to adolescents of other countries was unheard of here where life was bounded by tradition as old as the breezes that pass through the poplars in front of the church.

Nonetheless, they came, these foreign boys, in their twenties and thirties. They came from all over the world. But mainly they came from America and England. And by hook or by crook they found Morón. They found Diego and became almost, one could say, bewitched by the *falsetas*. Always they stayed longer than expected. Often three years would go by and history for them was recounted only in the number of *falsetas* earned and stored in the memory, scribbled down on scraps of paper stuffed in guitar cases and pockets, or recorded by secret tape recorders concealed in jackets during lessons and family fiestas.

Diego himself was known to have said, more than once, "These young foreigners, they act at fiestas as if they were in church!" A few young boys with talent were taken into the family. They were taught the authentic versions, the real material, whose roots extended beyond the town and found their source in the dry soil, the arches of the Roman bridges and stone *verias,* ancient paths.

Leslie was one of them. Another was Douglas Barnes, whom I met my first years there and who later taught me how to watch clouds to enliven the practice of scales. Doug was six-two and weighed on a good day perhaps 140 pounds. He could be seen walking slowly down the street, a cap covering his straight, slicked-back hair, and black sunglasses — the kind worn by the elderly Spaniards — covering his thin bug-face. Diego referred to Douglas as his fifth nephew. A distinction earned not by his technique on the guitar, though he was fastidious and practiced five hours a day along with the rest of us. Rather, it was earned by his ability to absorb the "air" of the music and to produce the necessary dryness of sound. It was said he had the air, "El tiene aire." A quality evaluated by the old ones who knew what brought the *duende* — the ghost's spirit — into a room. The *aire* could not be taught. In fact, some stayed in Morón for well over a decade and never achieved *aire,* but only more and more technique.

There was something in the receptivity of Doug's soul that enabled him to hear what was important in the music. He was not distracted by the acrobatic displays of almost mind-deceiving technique. Years later he told me that he would go after a *falseta* with a chisel in hand. Like a strange construction of an underground ice crystal, or the inner world of a geode, he would slowly begin to crack the mystery. After staying up all night listening to the repetition of one theme develop into complex variations, he would quietly ask the questions and find the key, over dawn cognac and coffee. How did that pause of silence occur in the fifth variation and return to the *compás*? What was the bridge?

A poignant story followed this young man, a story that I heard one night in the Bar Pepe. It seemed that Doug was a virgin when he arrived. Because of extreme thinness as a youth, that adolescent surge of springtime sensuality had left him behind. But the men in Morón did not judge sexuality by appearance. If you had form, if you had character, then you had *cojones*. Balls. And so one night, Diego, then in his early sixties, and several older compadres, extracted Douglas from his small dwelling where he was holed up with his tapes. No doubt they had dreamed this scheme up in Bar Pepe early that evening, and by one in the morning were convinced of the worth of their actions. Douglas was to see a whore that night.

There were three whores in town. Two older whores, whom everyone knew, and a young girl of about sixteen who had just recently begun. Of course, Douglas was to have the young one, and they took him trembling to her house on the outskirts of town. *"Resulta que"* (the expression in those parts that explained all causality) was that Douglas never left her house again. They sung his first love affair all summer long in the *bulerías*. She, too, was thin, and occasionally, one could glimpse their waif-like bodies strolling the promenade on a moonlit night.

One can stroll around the outskirts of a story in a similar fashion. There is the center of town where the action occurs, the outskirts of town where the shadow comes to life, and outside of town where the road leads over the hill.

I stepped off the bus one hot and dusty afternoon into the center of town. A young girl of sixteen. Alone. It's true, I've seen pictures — of me, standing in front of the green door, three doors up from Bar Pepe. I'm standing in a short, flowered skirt and a little red jersey top. My hands are folded in front of me like a good girl. But my legs are way too long. And my breasts are pushing out against my jersey top. There is something exposed and fragile that the girlish smile is trying to cover. It's hopeless, though. I couldn't cover my sexuality any more than the T-shirt could cover those breasts.

I stepped off the bus, the only foreigner among crowds of old women dressed in black and carrying chickens under their arms and baskets in their hands. A tall, lanky, dark Gypsy boy limped toward me, his leg dragging behind him like a stick. In Morón a bonding can occur which is immediate and serious. And in my case, it was Aurelio. "Yo quiero apprender la guitarra," I said to him, strumming the strings of an imaginary guitar. I had memorized those words on the plane from New York to Madrid, on the smaller plane to Sevilla and on the old hot bus to Morón. Those words had brought me halfway around the world. I want to learn to play the guitar.

He motioned back to me pantomiming the guitar. I followed Aurelio up the narrow street. Past the old church on the right and up around the corner. Before me was Plaza San Miguel — a small intimate plaza whose church slants its old eyes across the square, and whose five poplars move always with a hidden breeze. The old church slants upward toward the ancient castle, which is forever crumbling downwards. Limping a few feet ahead of me, Aurelio deposited me at the Bar Pepe. That cool darkened room. One room with a high ceiling. A few dominos tables. A bar for standing and drinking. One bathroom, for men. Two doors. One front. One side. A window. And the history of the *Cante*, the Song, soaked into the green walls.

As I walked down into the bar, a glass was thrown against the wall to signal the completion of a short round of dancing. All eyes were on Ansonini as he wove his body into a graceful and humorous gesture. This gesture, though brief, embodied the end of a five-year love affair with Rosa the Notorious.

Ansonini had at that time three teeth, shocking blue eyes, and an abundance of hair that lay like a mop on his head. His voice was like gravel and sent infants howling to their mothers. But when he sang, old men sobbed openly into their hands.

The glass seemed to crash not an inch from my head. It seemed that for this reason and no other, Ansonini took note of me. He took me under his enormous wing and brought me into the dim, unchanging light of the Bar Pepe.

I was christened La Gorda by Ansonini. This was supposedly because I was fat. However, what was never said was that it was my breasts, young and full, that were being honored.

Nothing less than a loss of my innocence could have catapulted me out of that community, that circle of warmth and protection. An adventure was conceived of innocently enough, as are all other creations, in the afternoon lull of Bar Pepe. Ansonini and José decided that we would take a trip to

Torremolinos to pick up Mary. Mary, a schoolteacher in her thirties, who had decided after one week with José to divorce her husband of ten miserable years, told me the first day I met her: "If it doesn't go another day, still it would be worth the pain." José, bartender at Bar Pepe, had a soothing effect on people. A nondescript character in comparison to those who swirled through the bar daily, he was the ears and eyes of this Gypsy community. More than that, he was a neutral ear. One of the few Gypsies in Morón who didn't make a judgment about every person and every act. For this reason all of us told him our stories, and he told no one.

Diez-y-ocho, an American boy named for the number "18" on the football jersey he always wore, was coerced into driving the van. And Ángel's silent uncle, Miguel, would chaperone the party. On the way we would stop to visit Ángel, Manuel's brother, a guitarist who was rumored to be able to make people vomit with the power of his *bulerías*.

It was Ángel's crossed eye that first charmed me as he opened the door. He was wearing cotton pajamas that looked like silk, or perhaps they were silk pajamas that looked like cotton. They slid off to one side of his shoulder, the way his eye slid toward his nose. His hair was long in front and dropped down over the one good eye. Disconcerting, but elegant.

He opened the door and in one hand he held a glass of cognac. In the other, his guitar. It was six in the morning. We had been traveling all night. As we climbed the steps to his apartment, one could hear the frantic notes. The high-strung *bulerías* and the driving *compás* moved from the A-chord to the B-flat and back. Reaching the door and opening it, Ángel stood there looking at me, with the eye looking inward and the pajama shirt sliding off the naked shoulder.

I had been warned in the car. During the long drive through the mountains I was told that Ángel had *guasa*. And that was the long and short of it. "What is *guasa?*" I asked, though I had already heard the word thrown about in heated arguments in the bars.

"*Guasa* is when you pull down your pants and shit on the street, in front of a public bar that houses a toilet inside," Pepe said, looking to Ansonini for approval. Ansonini chuckled. The silent uncle in the backseat of the van, wearing an old Panama, leaned forward in his seat. Diez-y-ocho drove on, nodding at what he didn't understand.

Evidently Ángel had performed this act of *guasa* during his *borrachera*, a drunken binge in Morón. This was what one might call obvious *guasa*, a form of intentional spite. But there is a continuum. *Guasa* can be quite subtle. And as with all things in Spain, there is an art to it. One of the more appealing aspects of *guasa* is the chance it affords people to air their philosophical views. For after each act of *guasa*, sure enough there would be a heated discussion in Bar Pepe among those involved as well as among onlookers. Was it, in fact, *guasa?* was always the first question to be addressed. An important diagnosis of the situation. Was it intentional? Was it without shame? Was it directed at the recipient? And after this initial round of discussion, there came an intricate description of what the *guasa* was. Its essence and then the details. And last, how the victim responded. More than likely, if the *guasa* was spicy, a fiesta would ensue. Some light *bulerías*, and perhaps the very *guasa* incorporated into a *letra*, a verse for the friends' amusement. If the *guasa* was grim and vicious, as it sometimes was, factions would develop. Each faction would go to its own bar to further discuss the insult. And then there would be several fiestas.

At first, it seemed to me strange that the perpetrator of *guasa*, though chastised, was secretly admired. But I soon realized that it was the opportunity for the community to judge, to debate, to evaluate the small nuances of daily life. The bar turned into an informal court of law. The deed in question was the crime, not the person.

The major artists in town set the tone of the crime. Diego's form of *guasa* was playful. And so too was his *bulerías*. Manuel's *guasa* was innocent; so too was his *bulerías*. Ángel's *guasa* was demonic. Though he was only a young man, he could reduce a person. And so too his *bulerías*. He had the respect of the town, although except for his immediate family, people kept their distance. But they waited for his visits to Morón with anticipation. "We don't want you to even look at him, *niña*," said Ansonini fondly. It was a setup.

"A big fish!" Those were the first words he said to me. "Un pescado grande. Un gran pescado." I was pulling off my T-shirt, bathing suit underneath, and stepping out of my skirt when he spoke. I thought he had been staring at me all morning, but with Ángel it was hard to tell. I ran down to the sea. I was exuberant with the Mediterranean. I was a young girl with my two friends, Ansonini and Ángel. I glanced back before plunging into the sea and saw them in the distance. Ansonini's old hat, bobbing in the heat, just barely visible.

"¿Quieres dormir conmigo?" Ángel asked, leaning close to my seat at the crowded table in the Gypsy quarter of the plaza. "Do you want to sleep with me?" I'm not sure how we got from the Mediterranean Sea to the Plaza in Torremolinos. But this I remember. After his big fish comment, Ángel had ignored me. I had tagged along after the three of them, through the teeming-with-tourists streets, until we reached a table for drinks in the Gypsy section of the plaza in the center of Torremolinos.

"What does that mean?" I asked Ansonini.

"¿Qué, niña?" he growled.

"¿Quieres dormir conmigo?" I repeated.

Ansonini's expression was closer to shock than I'd ever seen on that face of infinite emotion to which nothing human was foreign. "¡Conmigo!" he practically screamed.

"¡No!" Ángel leaned over, knocking his hat off. "Conmigo."

They glared at each other across my breasts. Suddenly I understood. I looked at Ansonini and I looked at Ángel. I've heard that your life is supposed to pass before you when you approach the moment of death, but I live to testify that my then short life passed before me in this moment of pure lust. "Yes," I said turning towards Ángel. "Quiero dormir contigo." And these were the first words I said to this man: I want to sleep with you.

"Bueno," he said and turned back to Pepe, continuing his conversation.

Plans were made, and as evening approached, the ebb and flow of Gypsies stopping to say hello thinned. Ángel excused himself to play at a *juerga,* a paid fiesta. We were to reconvene in the wee hours. Ansonini took my arm muttering, "¡Qué guasa! ¡Qué sinvergüenza!" What spite! What shamelessness! The uncle in the Panama trailed behind us and Diez-y-ocho circled at a distance as we continued our promenade through the town.

Scandal pursued me all the way back from Torremolinos across the high mountain pass, through Ronda and on to Morón. Unavoidable. Scandal flies on the wings of the crow, and onto the black hems of the dresses of the white-haired widows rocking back and forth to pass the long hot siesta hours. It seemed the story preceded me and had arrived by the time we returned. But how could I explain in my halting Spanish that we did not make love; that there were no beds available in any of the numerous sleeping seaport towns we aroused all the way down the coast. Who would have believed that the leering uncle in the backseat and Diez-y-ocho driving and Ángel and I laughing were all that occurred. When we finally reached the Rock of Gibraltar and Algeciras, Ángel and I had fallen exhausted and sweating onto a single bed into a deep sleep.

Even I had trouble standing firm behind my story during the long ride back among the knowing winks and nods of Ansonini, Diez-y-ocho, and the uncle who never uttered a word. I was in love with the laughter that our unspent passion had generated and mistook this for the deed itself. And as I waited all month for that laughter to return to Morón, embodied in the cross-eyed Gypsy boy of my dreams, the scandalous adventure simmered on the back burner of gossip that brewed constantly at Bar Pepe, erupting in full force the day Ángel arrived a month later.

I knew he was due and was warned by my dear friend, Ansonini, that the laughing boy of my dreams was really a cross-eyed demon. There are certain lessons that can never and will never be transmitted from the old to the young. Lessons in love are to be lived out to the bitter end. By the time I entered Bar Pepe at one in the afternoon, Ángel, who had arrived that afternoon, was already in the midst of a full scale *borrachera*. Unknown to me, I had wounded his pride in Algeciras and he was ready to catch the big fish once and for all, under the approving eyes of his compadres. I should have sensed that he had turned mean from the way the tone of his voice had turned into a sneer, and the rapid change of his charm to mockery. But my longing for the return of laughter was so great that I overlooked the all-too-clear signs of approaching *guasa* of the darkest variety. Years later I still tried to explain my blindness as youthful naïveté, but the sad truth of the matter is that even now my longing for this form of laughter obscures my vision at crucial times. And so the scandalous crow pursues me in adulthood.

Ángel invited me to drink at one bar and then another. Each one taking us further from town. Each one more remote. At each bar I kept pace with his drinking to be polite until I was stumbling blind and incoherent through the back alleyways of Morón farther and farther from the protective eye of *la gente,* ever watchful as a Greek chorus.

The smell of anisette still makes me as sick as I felt when Ángel, laughing, grabbed my purse and left me to vomit on a dusty nameless corner of a squalid barrio. By the time I arrived back at the Plaza San Miguel it was dark. My knees were bleeding and my stockings torn. Barefoot, shoes in hand, I crept up the stairs to the left of the bar, avoiding being seen, but hearing the life and the music ooze through the walls and out into the night. Suddenly I felt on the outside, as clearly and definitively as I had felt earlier that day on the inside of the vitality that held us all in its light.

I crept up the stairs to my one-room apartment three doors up from Bar Pepe. The texture of my sleep that night I will never forget. Weeping and moaning, I was sick over and over again, and my body too paralyzed even to roll to the side of the bed. I was shaken awake from semi-delirium by Mary. A family trial of sorts was in the making and I was the key witness. With Mary's aid I made my way to the Bar Pepe.

The family was assembled, all in formal attire; suits and ties and pressed dresses, the parents, Ángel, Manuel, and the two sisters. The purse in question was ceremoniously returned to me by Ángel under the stern gaze of the parents. Yes. It was mine. And though it was clearly snatched by the eldest son, Ángel, it was just as clear by the coldness of the shoulders that *la culpa era mía.* That famous Morón phrase. The fault was mine. Had I not allowed myself to be in a position for the deed to occur?

This was the first time I felt alien. This was not an American court of law. And the consequences were as devastating as they were unforeseen. I was shunned. I walked out of the bar with my purse in hand but my head hanging low. There was a shock here, and it was not the last time I was to feel its waves. As close as I had become to this family, I was still an outsider. In short, I was not Gypsy. And *la culpa* therefore would always be mine. A form of original sin. To be born non-Gypsy with the love of flamenco running through my veins.

And this is where Leslie first entered my life. That there were other foreigners living within the family in Morón was a fact I had not really taken into account. I had seen them on the periphery like shadows following the light, but I had not acknowledged their presence or their relationship to me. "They are different" was all I had to tell myself to ignore them. But as I fell out of one circle of protection, I fell into another. I, too, became an outsider looking in and this position had its own special gifts. The outsider on the outskirts has a unique slant on the truth. The light shifts slightly and the picture changes focus.

Leslie and I, for example, were two lost English-speaking children searching for *falsetas* to bring us home. And when Leslie put his hand in mine, already knowing about the purse scandal in detail, I knew that we were kin.

"I'll take you to the hut," Leslie offered. "And we'll spend the night there away from the watchful eyes and ears of the bar."

Feeling that I was forever to be non-Gypsy, I had made plans to leave the next morning for the States. My three year stay had come to a crashing halt. It was only on my next trip to Morón that I realized still another layer of the truth. With my scandal, I had entered the history of the *Cante*. A lively verse for the *bulerías* had been created in my honor:

Una judía de los Estados Unidos
Una niña se llama La Gorda
le dió su corazón y su bolsa
a un gitano muy sin vergüenza

A Jewess from the United States
A child called The Fat One
Gave her heart and her purse
To a Gypsy with no shame

During that night in the hut with this lonely English boy I earned a treasure worthy of my misadventure. The hut itself was a white, crumbling, old adobe structure standing alone at the nape of a vast valley where mountains, outlined purple and mauve in the growing light, rose on all sides. It had been Tuerto's.

It was here that Tuerto had created his forlorn *soleá*. The one room was desolate and dirty, with soiled sheets on the single bed and old discarded tins of sardines half-burnt in the ashes of the fire hole. And so here I had my first guitar lesson from a non-Gypsy. Leslie had no *compás* and less *aire*. But his loneliness was as large as the mountains surrounding the hut and his need for the music provided its own *compás*. The rings of grief were believable in the aging dawn.

With almost no technique he struggled through his desperate *soleá*. I had not heard the last *falseta* before. Not at any of the baptisms, barroom afternoons or all-night fiestas. It was one of the rare and secret *falsetas* of Tuerto, never played in public — Leslie had procured it through long hard hours of serious hanging out with the old drunk. It was as forlorn and beautiful as a winter's star. And its melody burned into my memory, accompanying me on my departure the next afternoon as I stepped back onto a hot and dusty bus, alone as I had come.

It became my song of departure and as such it stood me well until my next return to that baked white pueblo in the olive-treed mountains outside of the city, Sevilla.

And so Rafael learned how I had come to know Tuerto's secret *falseta*. He had listened to my tale and now we sat slumped together in a heap, the night no longer young and the bottle of cognac emptied to the drop. "Es verdad," Rafael pronounced with a solemn nod. It is true. From that moment on that he claimed to have been in the shoebox with me right from birth.

So began my *bulerías* education, though not a note had been exchanged. There was no better way to begin. All *falsetas* worth the learning begin with a story lived and end with the telling of its tale.

PART TWO

Bulerías

Song of Sensuality

Chapter 6

Doug's solo tape is more beautiful than any I have heard, short of Diego's himself. I wish you could hear it as I have tonight, coming home to my empty apartment in Berkeley. I can hear in each song the years of my lessons. It confirms my musical quest in a way that my trips to Spain did not. I wonder at these journeys, mine and others. These musical quests. I have wondered if my time has been well spent. Or better yet, if my time has been well wasted.

I spent no less than a year studying what I have named the Bulerías Bridge. When I first heard it leap out at me in a lesson I believed that I had discovered it. And indeed, I did. Each discovery is the original moment, fresh with optimism and excitement. What made Doug's *bulerías* unique? What made his *bulerías* connect the loneliness of the *soleá por bulerías* with the pulse of the *bulerías por soleá?* That was the question I brought to my lesson.

I was answered with the Bridge. Six beats connecting the end of one twelve with the beginning of the next twelve. A syncopation of the third beat that stretched out like the San Franscisco Bay Bridge connecting two bodies of land. That syncopation bridged a gap between the ending of one twelve and the beginning of a new twelve. A gap bridger that suspends time between the end and the beginning with an accent toward the fresh phrase. This accent catapults you into the start of the new, almost at the same moment it is pulling you back toward the old. It is a leap.

"Teach me that," I almost yelled, as the awareness of its existence articulated out of pure kinesthetic response into consciousness.

Doug's eyebrows raised in acknowledgment and a small smile came to his face. "So now you've heard the connector, have you? I better watch out for my soul. You don't miss a thing."

It's not that he had kept it secret from me. It was mine once I heard it. But as with all flamenco lessons, until the moment of hearing, the door remains closed. *Falsetas* were exchanged always. But the wisdom within the *falseta* is like the meaning within a plot. Without that wisdom, the *falsetas* are plot with no substance.

I worked on the connecting bridge for at least a year. I had to learn how to fit it into the *compás*. First thing every morning next to the bed, I'd click on the tape of Doug playing those six beats over and over. Last thing before sleep. I played it up, down and around. I was patient, and in a year it was mine. I had the patience of a saint, when it came to learning that music. Patience and faith. I wonder where those qualities have gone now that I need them?

The gap between this old wisdom and my own culture seems too great to bridge with only six beats. This gap yawns open like the Grand Canyon of the soul. I am hanging in the syncopation, waiting for the courage to leap.

It seems that no one in Andalusia, as yet, has lost home. For this I am envious. All over the world, in the most unexpected places, American rock and roll blares out its message. Except in Andalusia. In Andalusia, you are likely to hear Antonio Mairena wailing his *cante* in a taxi cruising the early dawn streets of Morón. Here the message still travels from the old to the young.

Is it possible that the rain in Morón is older than anywhere else in the world, or is it just the way it falls here on these narrow streets of old stone? Watching it fall from Bar Pepe, I wonder how many hours and years of my life I could spend thinking about this.

Several men stand in the doorway. They too are watching. But it seems that they are also waiting. Manuel waits. The old men still call him *niño*. And watching him wait and the rain fall, I can see him an old man, still in the same posture. I can see his father's face in his, and perhaps the only difference will be which lines deepen and which do not.

The buildings smell like earth after a good rain. You could be waking up on a farm. That brown-green smell. One difference though. Here, there is a musky smell. Just as, on a farm, you have the sweet strong smell of horses and hay mixed with earth, so here in Morón one smells the age of the buildings. Out of the stone, the smell of earth and dust.

The way Manuel gets up in the morning is like this. First he pulls himself to a sitting position. He's a big man, much larger than most Gypsies, and now he's put on weight. We were both sixteen when we first met and Manuel was as thin as a guitar string. But about his getting up. He drags himself to a sitting position and then puts his socks on and then his black, shined shoes. He is very nearsighted and has to hold the shoes close to his eyes in order to untie last night's knots. Even though it's not cold anymore. It's May, but he is so used to the tiled floors chilling his blood that he takes no chances. The shoes go on first, before the underwear.

The reason that the rain is so comforting here is that it seems all right to be sad. The buildings and the roads weep. The olive trees weep. The churches and the fountains. It seems that the weeping is not coming from me, but moving in from the outside.

Where I live in California, people don't believe in tragedy. And because of that, or who knows which way it started, the buildings there don't weep. The new age is searching for a back door to paradise. There is a relentless blue sky.

Katerina says that you can't live in Morón simply because you love the color of the buildings. She says it's not enough. "See it for what it is. You're being overromantic." Yet she's been here for fifteen years and now only wears shades of browns and reds. The color is bleached blood against sun-starched white. This brown-red drips down the buildings; my blood rushes on to meet itself.

In Morón, the rain is perceived as a time to rest. Umbrellas are mended with patience. Manuel threaded the miniscule eye of the needle with black thread that he kept in the left top drawer of his dresser expressly for this purpose. With focused attention he mended, breathing lightly through the nose, as some who concentrate are prone to do. Manuel worked for Mateo's father, who was an umbrella mender. "One umbrella should last a lifetime" was his motto. And they often did. Big, old, black umbrellas appear in the afternoon, like crows, pecking their way along the stone streets.

Mateo's father is dead now, and so Manuel continues to sew late into the morning. The birds can be heard raising voices one layer under the rain. The rain moves down through layers of sound.

Mateo and Katerina lived together for seven years. They could be seen arguing in the market every Saturday morning. The Gypsy and the German. Katerina takes the love of stone to a degree beyond the known continuum. Her stoicism knows no bounds. One summer day in Sevilla, suffering the heat in her apartment, I made what seemed to be an obvious suggestion.

"Let's buy a fan," I said to Katerina. It was 110 degrees with 90 percent humidity. That summer, according to weather historians, was the worst in over a hundred years. In comparison, New York summers seemed cooler, cooled by coastal breezes.

Katerina looked at me indignantly and said, "Quiero solamente aire puro." I want only pure air, is what she said.

She could have said this in any one of the five languages she spoke, and that she chose to exclaim her indignation in Spanish added emphasis to her point. And so we suffered. The truth is, I suffered and Katerina remained immune.

It may have been her early years in the war that gave Katerina the ability to drink any Gypsy under the table, to outwalk a donkey, to smoke two packs of unfiltered cigarettes a day, and to stay up two and three days running with only a sweet in the morning. Katerina once confided in me about her early years.

A few days before the war began, her mother gave her a chocolate. "Eat this, my dear," she said. "For this is the last sweet you will have for ten years to come." Potato soup was what she ate for the next ten years, as she stood in food lines, on the run from town to town. To this day, the smell of potato makes her sway with nausea. It is only her teeth, however, that show the signs of early malnutrition.

It was coincidental, I think, that Mateo became famous because of his teeth. And potato soup, I am sure, had little to do with his case. One Saturday morning, after market, I was having a *copa* with Katerina, Mateo, and Manuel. Manuel turned toward me and said, "Have you seen Mateo's teeth?"

I thought this question must have been a form of early-morning *guasa*, for we had all seen Mateo's teeth. The top row stuck straight out, perpendicular from his mouth. At a loss for words, I looked dumbly toward Katerina, who glanced mischievously at Mateo. Mateo took his cheek in hand and pulled back the upper lip away from the gum.

Underneath the full row of perpendicular teeth was another row of long, but otherwise normal, teeth.

"¡Otra copa!" Katerina pronounced and so another round of drinks was ordered.

Taking issue with Katerina is a serious matter. I remain convinced that she tried to kill me one summer in Portugal. From the start, Katerina had not wanted to drive. Her real desire was to walk from Sevilla to Portugal. And it was from a position of appeasement that I had agreed against my better judgment to walk through las Bastiques, the highest and oldest mountains on the border of Spain and Portugal.

There were no peasants out in the field that day. Not even a burro. All the burros were safely holed up in the cool of their darkened stone sheds. Temperatures were close to 120 degrees, with no wind to be felt. It was *la calena.* The white sky. *La calena.* The word was on the lips of all the peasants who were slowly shaking their heads as they passed each other, clinging to the shady side of the street on the way to market. "*La calena*" was uttered knowingly, directly after the expected "*Buenos,*" and with a slow nods of the head.

It was on this day that we set out. I had promised and I was not one to renege. We had a small argument before we were out of the pueblo. Katerina insisted that we take no water. "There will be plenty of water in the mountains," she said. And as for a map, the idea did not appeal to Katerina's judgment. A judgment based solely on aesthetics. "Hay verias" is all Katerina would say. There were ancient stone paths that led through the mountains. They were good enough for the peasants for over a thousand years, and they would be good enough for us. And so we began. No food. No water. No hats. No maps.

I had never known mountains that had no breeze. That had no sound. That did not gather coolness at the top. The only sound was that of the flies, buzzing away the afternoon, seeming to take up what little was left of the air. The pine trees were so dry and dusty and so close together that moving through them was difficult. The olive trees were scorched and desolate. "¡Dónde estamos!" Katerina yelled suddenly, into the silent mountains, whose age seemed actively to mock the lifespan of one individual.

Katerina had spotted three peasants, who could be seen on the horizon across the next valley. "¿Dónde está la cima?" Katerina yelled over and over again. "Where is the top?" It was then that I realized that neither of us knew which way was up and which way was down. We were lost. On that point there was no debate. It was at this moment that I took issue with Katerina.

"I'm thirsty," I said. "Tengo sed." I said this with defiance and with malice. We had been out for five hours, with no water. It was high noon. Every stream was dry. "I'm thirsty," I said to Katerina, daring her to do something about it.

Katerina looked at me in disgust. She got down on her hands and knees and scavenged two small smooth stones out of the hard ground. One rock she popped in her mouth. "Suck on a rock," she said to me. "It will keep you from your thirst." She deposited the other stone in my mouth.

It was my anger at Katerina, and not the stone, that kept

me going. For the next ten hours we did not exchange a word. When we reached the first stream, the moon was well up, and in the distance one could see the rooftops of the next pueblo, which had been rumored to be only three hours away by foot.

I fell into the stream face first and began to drink, when I noticed that Katerina was squatting just upstream from me. "Katerina, for god's sake, what are you doing! This is good drinking water."

Katerina looked at me with a wry smile. "Niña," she said, "thirty goats peed in this stream just five minutes before you arrived."

"¡Tu! Tu eres una cabre alemana," I said with no humor intended. You are a German goat.

A year later, Katerina wrote me a letter. She told me that I challenge the source in people. She said: "Loren, you are still so vehemently on my mind!"

Chapter 7

The fact that I lost four teeth in Spain is irreversible. But among friends, that's status. Mica has a scar on her arm where Fernanda bit her in the throes of affection: predawn fiesta, 1962. This also counts as status. Doug has a picture of himself drinking sherry out of Fernanda's high-heeled shoe: early morning postfiesta, 1968.

It's not hard to gain notoriety in the flamenco community, but the criteria are mysterious. And more mysterious still is the question of what kind of collective mentality defines the rules. My friend Ira, who is a rock and rhythm guitarist, claims that the flamenco world is nothing more than a nasty clique, designed to exclude people. He says that art has nothing to do with the backbiting ins and outs of flamenco etiquette. I don't argue with him.

I don't want to present an overromanticized version of my Gypsy friends. They are sometimes horrible. And the flamenco scene? Cutthroat. It's not just the particular brand of spite that is the Gypsies' own; it's also the foreigners that are drawn to them. As moths to the light. Often one is shoulder to shoulder at a bar with a most shadowy character, buying drinks for precisely the kind of person one has been taught to avoid. Bad company! I often go incognito in Andalusia. Even my friends — the ones with the real "sentido para el arte," feeling for the art — even they are capable of extraordinary malice for the sake of the music.

That I spent twenty years becoming an expert at maneuvering my way into the fiestas, displaying my impressive knowledge of *falseta* history, does not shame me. But then "having no shame" is considered a virtue. I have spent long hours discussing the appropriateness of actions that nowhere else in the world would be given two minutes of thought.

"I have only been playing guitar for two years," says one guitarist to another, whose *toque* suggests no less than ten years of hard practice.

"And I just began to practice *picado* two months ago," retorts another virtuoso.

"I was born with prenatal *compás*," I insist, and this statement temporarily ends a long argument in yet another scintillating barroom debate.

I contend that this debate is really no different than the age-old dialectic concerning good works and grace. It is also my belief that all over the globe people discuss basically the same things dressed in the small details of local life. Really, there are only a few conversations with an infinite number of variations.

There is a belief, or shall I say superstition, among flamenco guitarists that runs deep. One is either born into *compás* or not. "That which is Gypsy is found in the grooves of the hands and the lines of the face," is the Andalusian quotation thrown in to support this notion. The birth of Paco de Lucia, considered by many to be the greatest guitarist, of the twentieth century at least, has thrown a wrench into this notion of grace. Paco is non-Gypsy. Yet clearly he has *compás.* If his twelve hours of practice a day created this condition then it was "good works" that played a hand in his genius? "Is a guitarist born or made?" is what it boils down to. Are hearts had as a gift, or are they earned?

I have seen guitarists and aficionados come to blows over the issue of Paco de Lucía. I saw this in Bar Pepe. Even in my own home in California. Not only does Paco's prowess touch off this age-old argument between the Catholics and Protestants around grace; Paco has become the symbol of urban flamenco. Paco has moved flamenco into the modern world, by allowing other rhythms and instruments to penetrate the sacred archetypes of form. This is no small matter. Even I, when it was late enough and I was drunk enough, have felt like slugging someone who'd suggest that Paco's *toque* is stronger than Diego's.

The underlying theme in this always-heated discussion is the concept of "purism" in art. That Diego's art was and is "pure" is never under debate. It stands in its totality, a singular statement, unencumbered by the world that even then was groaning toward its technological fate. Diego's art had tragedy. But it was the tragedy of the soul, not the cry of the soulless. To claim that Paco de Lucía is stronger, *tiene más fuerza,* than Diego del Gastor is not simply a matter of taste.

It is a statement of philosophy. It is a statement of ethics. It is nothing short of a belief system.

It is difficult to resist the temptation to divide the world between those who like modern flamenco and those who cherish the *arte puro*. And it is here that my friend's criticism pierces the heart. "Music is for everyone," he rightly pronounces. "Why shouldn't anyone who wants to, play at a fiesta? Why shouldn't flamenco be mixed with other instruments and styles? What's so sacred?"

In other words, how far should one go to protect what does not exist any more? The pure art in its natural habitat. The kitchen. The bar. The *venta*. And what extreme actions are valid in its name's sake? Where do you draw the line between "honoring" and "exclusivism" for its own sake? These questions at first glance may appear to be academic. But they are the source of real actions in the world.

Many a good person starting out on his or her search has become embittered toward flamenco. With all good intentions one might believe she was at a fiesta to listen to music, find herself instead embroiled in a violent debate about the world as seen through this one's *falseta* or that one's *letra*.

At times I have been called into action, and in a moment have had to make split-second decisions that affect the well-being of another person. I am ashamed to tell you that I once excluded two perfectly decent people, who happened to be my friends, from a potential fiesta. Why? Simply because they were foreign and someone whom I thought was an expert in measuring the delicate atmosphere of *gusto* in a Gypsy group said "no more foreigners."

I wince, even to myself, remembering how Katerina and I sped through the back alleyways of a small pueblo in her Citroën in an effort to lose those two American friends — whom I had actually invited for the evening — only to almost run them over at a treacherous blind intersection. "Tell them there's no room in the car," Katerina ordered. I obeyed shamelessly, as I watched them limp off to the bus station, wretched and demoralized. Tortured, I knew, by the thought that they would miss the really profound moment, though we'd already heard eight straight hours of music. We had all followed Luis Fuentes, as he literally danced through the streets, his white scarf flying and his song picking up strays at every bar — taxi drivers who knew how to sing the *Cante* and young Gypsy boys who could clap *siguiriyas* flawlessly.

"That was only a warm-up," is the way it would be presented the next day in the bar.

As it turned out, the rest of the evening, even after screening out the Americans, was dismal. From this fiesta, I learned a lesson of great flamenco import. Never choose the music over friendship. Somewhere down the road your own *guasa* will come back on you, double. As I am a late bloomer when it comes to wisdom, I am not too hard on myself. But also, I had been up all night, smoking strong cigarettes and drinking bad wine. This interfered with my judgment. *Lo juro.* I swear it!

The setting is a small barrio, a neighborhood outside Sevilla. It's not what you'd expect from books. We have dumped my friends, the other Americans, and Katerina and I are waiting. The barrio is poor. And we are sitting in a small cement bar, located in the middle of a housing project. The temperature is no less than 100 degrees. Why are we here? We have brought together Luis Fuentes, one of the only authentic flamenco dancers of "the younger generation," and La Madre, an older Gypsy woman in her seventies, who, according to my friend Katerina, is a secret phenomenon of the arte. Katerina has literally dedicated her life to this form of knowledge, so I don't question her.

We have been up all night at a festival in Utrera, where Luis performed for money. He did not dance well at all. This man is only at home in his art, dancing in local bars for his friends. He has never been able to step onto the stage. *¿Resulta que?* He is starving in Lebrija. And to make matters worse, his butcher shop has been replaced by a supermarket! Last week he went to see a psychiatrist who put him on antidepressants. It is difficult to imagine: Luis Fuentes on antidepressants.

La Madre cannot afford the three dollars necessary for *entrada al festival.* So we have brought Luis to her. She has scurried off to call her friends. We wait in the darkened bar. The street outside is blank with heat and cement. I think to myself, "this will be the *fiesta del cementerio.*"

Taxis begin to pull up in front of the bar. An old man with a cane. A thin man with dark sunglasses. An obese woman wearing a scarf. None under seventy. Each makes his or her entrance into the bar, embraces Luis, and before too long, tears have begun to flow, and many rounds of wine have been ordered. Each is an artist.

Katerina is whispering the legendary histories of each entrance fervently in my ear. "¡Escuche bien!" she says in her harshest Spanish with her thick German accent. Listen! Then she notices that I am falling asleep standing up, with my head propped on the bar. I take refuge in the bathroom, thinking to splash some cold water on my face. No such luck! The bathroom wins the award for *el peor del mundo.* The world's worst. A toilet growing, as it were, out of the wall. The seat too high to sit on. And shit splattered all over the walls. I reel back into the bar.

"¡Lorea!" Katerina commands me. "Ven acá muy pronto."

Conditions seem optimal for possibly one of the best fiestas of all time. Family and friends. A reunion of sorts. Already tears and exhaustion. Luis is *a gusto.* How does he do it? He's been up for two days and not a sign of fatigue.

Everything is perfect. A spread of food on the table. Olives, bread, oil, salami. And last but not least, that edge of discomfort that seems to be a precondition for good flamenco music. It can be either physical or emotional. In this case, the heat was unbearable, our sweat soaking the stale, hard bread. "One way to eat it," I am thinking when — "¡Vamos!" — the music starts. Luis is singing La Madre's favorite verse, and yes, her gigantic form is rising, rising, rising up off the chair to dance. I am thinking that it is worth all the trouble after all. Katerina looks as if she has swallowed a secret.

Just as the music hits its stride, the streets fill with a swarm of kids playing radios, blaring American rock and roll. The fiesta is over.

They can go very right and they can go very wrong, these fiestas. A wrong fiesta can put you out of sorts for weeks. So I tell myself the day after: "Be careful! Know your fiesta beforehand." But in a way, this is a contradiction in terms. Another contradiction lies in the aftermath. Whether the fiesta was good or bad, holy or profane, the next day is treacherous. And in some ways the better the fiesta was, the worse the reentry back into the world. If the fiesta was bad, one feels a lingering depression that spreads itself out over the weeks. But the next day is simple fatigue. There is no crashing back into the everyday world.

The morning of Mica's fiesta, there was a steely blue sunrise. Not warm and fleshy. A chill to turn one's collar up against. Cold drizzle. But still a brilliant blue in the east. The purple flowers around the house appeared to be ultraviolet. In Spain, one can stand near the warm smoke of the *churro* stands. Hot, steaming chocolate. Fried, dewy doughnuts made of potatoes. Manuel set the record, eating close to a pound of them one morning after a particularly tense fiesta.

It was the month of September. The leaves had begun to turn gold. And finally the breeze had cooled, after a summer that baked the mud into the hides of the burros. Even the flies had been pressed for air. Summer was over in one night, as suddenly as it had begun. It was over. We wore sweaters the night of Mica's fiesta. The night before that, I had been lying naked on the red-tiled floor in Manuel's apartment. The sheets were soaked so thoroughly with sweat I had hung them out to dry.

At the end of a fiesta, the sunrise is to be achieved. Those who play the guitar, but not well enough to perform, have their moment then. The morning of Mica's fiesta I played *bulerías*. My *golpe* was stronger than I would have imagined. A hoof coming down on the dusty ground. Hollow and dry.

The *golpe* keeps track of the *compás*. The third finger strikes the wood on the guitar face. It is not random. In the *bulerías*, the finger strikes down on the three, the six, the eight and the ten. It becomes the undertow. The pull against the rhythm.

Rafael's *golpe* sends dust off the strings. He says that he has a special wood under his golpe plate that creates this sound. I think not. I believe it to be in his hands. The *golpe* of the *bulerías* is relentless. It keeps coming. Rafael's *golpe* has something of the surf in it also. The thud of the waves as they roll in on a grey day. This he combines with the hollow hoofbeat. How he does this is one of his mysteries. The dull pounding of the surf with the dry hollow hoofbeat.

The fiesta at Mica's house ran for seven hours without a lull. After Rafael's last *bulerías*, the room hummed. No one wanted to leave. People sat quietly keeping company with one another. No one wanted to return to the singularity of their life. To the single bed. To the nuclear family. To the small town.

There is a great staying power in this music. And yet what seemed as if it would last a lifetime, Rafael's *bulerías* for example, leaves you wanting at the week's end. Like good sex, satisfaction and need are simultaneous and equal.

The morning after hearing Rafael play an original *bulerías*, I woke up with the movements of his face imprinted on my soul like a lover's head on a pillow recently vacated. "Unspeakable" is what a friend of mind said who had never heard flamenco before, her face suddenly broken with tears. Now just a short week later, I am needing the unspeakable song again.

Freud was wrong when he said creativity is repressed sexuality. In fact, sexuality is repressed guitar playing. O Rafael. Nothing else will do. Not sex. Not eating. Not sleeping.

"This could become a habit," I worry to myself, as if I'd not already become addicted. "Como una droga," they say in Spain. Just striking those strings. Moving through those chords.

Chapter 8

Douglas Barnes has told me on more than one occasion the reason he'd disappeared that six months in 1978 was directly related to my insatiable appetite for his *aire.* I was voracious. Every weekend I would drive the three hours to his retreat in Cloverdale, where he lived in a crumbling down old Victorian mansion on a secluded hill to devour more of him and his seemingly endless knowledge of *falsetas.*

My lessons would begin at any time, depending upon when Doug would wake from one of his several naps during the day. I almost hesitate to say "day," because in the world of Doug Barnes, time measurements like days and evenings were not relevant. When he first walked down the stairs into the large living room where torn red velvet curtains hung from floor to ceiling, I heard a slow and steady ticking that felt as if it were coming from inside a deep cavern, and yet also appeared to be a moving surface. I said to Doug, "What's ticking?"

He said, "Me."

Doug lost his heart in Morón. An infection in an abscessed tooth reached all the way down to his heart. He woke one morning with a premonition that he would die if he did not leave Morón and head for home. Two days later he arrived in L.A., and was carried off the plane on a stretcher.

He's been an invalid ever since. You can hear his heart ticking, like a stopwatch, when you walk into a room. Doug does a good deal of cloud watching, and this is surprising. Cloud watching is like bird watching. Both require a belief in a long life. Having been told that he would not live past forty, and now being forty two, one might think that Doug would not have time for this fruitful hobby.

It is an activity for birds. And Doug's heart, though enlarged three times the normal size, has wings nonetheless. Today while watching Doug practice, I learned an important clue. Every ten minutes or so he would stop and look out the window for several minutes. I asked him what he was doing.

Doug said, "Resting." His heart ticked quietly. "My hands tire, and so I rest," he said.

Each time he came back to the strings, when he drew his attention away from the clouds, back inward, the *falseta*, his original variation, developed, and the tone deepened.

I'll learn patience yet. I've studied with Doug for five years now. In fact, I've taken on so much of his quality, his *aire*, that another guitarist said to me, "Loren, your hands look like Doug's." That long rolling stride.

But that was just the beginning. It was not just his heart that made him seem a walking relic. Doug had several small suitcases made of old leather. Inside each of these carrying cases lived a small world of treasures. Each one older and more beautiful than the next. In neat compartments lived all the necessities for a singular life. A gold pocket watch obtained in an Andalusian flea market. Pen and paper of modest size. Two or three rare flamenco tapes. One or two extraordinary books. Just the ones you'd take to a deserted island. Several small foreign boxes, whose contents ranged from rare rocks and shells to a steady supply of different colored pills for a severe heart condition. Blindfolds for sleeping at any time of the day or night and earplugs for the same purpose. Saverez super-high tension strings and an old *cejia* from Cordoba.

Some of the cases contained only tapes. Or only shells. Or only books. Along the walls of his room were what seemed to be ancient pictures, yellowing at the corners, of groups of old men and women in formal outfits, sitting around tables filled with wine glasses and ashtrays. Singing. The one young man is always Doug. Thin even then, wearing dark glasses, with hair combed straight back off the head.

Doug knew the names of each shell, each rock, each tape. In fact, there seemed to be no end to the names he knew. But his greatest treasure was the rarest collection of old flamenco tapes, which he had procured from all the lost hours of fiestas and baptisms in Bar Pepe. He had recorded the history of the *falsetas*. He had the walls of Bar Pepe inside his old leather suitcases. When he wasn't napping, when he wasn't practicing, he was retaping, one by one, the original tapes. It was a race against time. Some of the tapes were dissolving into dust. When I understood the importance of the race, I understood why Doug never left his room.

In exchange for my lessons, I brought Doug blank tapes. And I received not only *falsetas*, but also history lessons. I was given the history of how the *falseta* was earned, as well as the story of its long journey through the generations.

"*Falsetas* live in the air," Doug said. "They congregate in small plazas. They are at home in the night."

Listening to La Fernanda sing *bulerías* this morning on a clean edited tape — with the nuances of Diego's *toque* as bright as morning sunshine — made me feel that perhaps Doug's project was all right after all. How it would stand up in a Gypsy court, I could guess. At worst he would be tried as a war criminal. At best, he would be sued for millions that he doesn't have, to make up for the millions that they, the Gypsies, have lost.

That Doug was the focus of this, the ultimate of controversies, is an irony of its own. We know that in exchange for Diego's pure *falsetas*, and the largest secret tape collection in all of flamenco history, he lost his heart in Morón. Was it, in the end, a fair exchange? Only Doug can answer that question for sure. It was a costly exchange. It was an even exchange. Life for death. Death for life. Do any of us really exchange any less?

Perhaps it is no surprise that it was Doug who decided to reverse the primary, unspoken but ever-present law of the great tradition of taping: "Thou shalt not make copies of, or sell, original tapes." On the eve of his approaching death, when even his friends didn't know he had already lost all feeling in his right arm, Doug decided to edit the tapes that had sat undisturbed in his suitcase for twenty years, and sell them to the ever-hungry, shifting, anonymous aficionados.

There is another unspoken law of the great tradition that is equal and entirely opposite to the above. It goes something like this: "We, the aficionados, will do everything we can to secretly record spontaneous fiestas and abscond with the tapes."

Our friends, the Gypsies, know this and attempt to trick us or catch us at every turn. I have known guitarists purposely to play bad or meaningless *falsetas* at the very whiff in the air of a machine in the room. On the other hand, I have known artists who were secretly glad after a fiesta that someone, unknown to them, had taped. One thing is for sure: I have never been to a fiesta without an argument erupting about taping. No matter how clear the agreement beforehand, once the event is set in motion, other forces come to bear, and performance is at least as large as possession.

The doctor has given Doug no more than two years to live. The sense of urgency continues. We have bought the best tape machine, and he is now editing and transferring all of Diego's tapes onto the best cassettes. Also he has taken on the arduous task of translating all the *letras* off the tape. That is, he will translate even the most drunken of the Andalusian toothless *cante*. He goes about his work in the stealth of night. He is a detective of sorts, though he never leaves his bed now at all. Mercedes is often there with him though she does not speak much these days. She attends to Doug. She brings him food. She cleans his place. She sits on his bed as if it were a great lawn spreading out before her. Last night I had dinner with Mercedes. I was worried about her. She assured me that when she sits on Doug's bed, she's at home.

I first got to know Mercedes in Spain, though I had first met her in California. From the start I was mystified by two elements. First, Mercedes has a perfectly petite body. She is as small as one can be without being an oddity. Her tiny body is at once so strong and so fragile that one feels a sense of awe around this perfect balance. She is a dancer and an athlete, and so the tone of her body glows, all ninety pounds of it. Also there is another quality that sends off this glow around her, and that is her purity of heart. Someone once said that purity of heart is the ability to will one thing. And this certainly is the case with my friend Mercedes. I should not have been at all surprised that she fell deeply in love with Doug. He is probably the only other person I know who has this same form of purity. You can hear the power of it in his every *falseta*. In every roll of *compás*. Both are quiet and shy. Both are thin and frail. Both have purity of heart and a power of concentration like the engine of a train barreling across the plains of Montana.

Mercedes assured me last night that she had temporarily overcome her grief about Doug's coming death. Mine has just begun. It has been hard to visit him recently, as I cannot bear to see him in pain. He is not depressed, which disproves the theory that without family or money one is alone as he approaches death. Doug is surrounded by neither family nor money. He now lives in a small one-room apartment around the corner from me. Within this room is his shell collection, his watch collection, his pictures of Spain, his huge collection of succulents, an Oscar fish (and every book written about said fish), his tape collection, several tape recorders, a six-inch TV, and the bed, which is simply a foam double mattress on the floor. The kitchen is in the adjacent room and contains an icebox, a small stove, a rudimentary sink, with a bathroom off to the side. Doug only sees one visitor a day, in order to conserve energy. There is always a waiting list.

His idea of editing the Diego tapes is a new one. It is an idea I wholeheartedly approve of. It will cause waves in the flamenco community at large. There is no end to the debate about whom this music belongs to. The deep song belongs to no one and to everyone. Diego has the right to his own music. It belongs to him and his family. But it's not their tradition to preserve fiestas. Doug spent most of his life collecting these tapes, and his is a larger task. It is archeology. He will mine each tape. He will translate the *letras*. He will tell the story of each fiesta.

There is a dialogue that was meant to go on one's whole life. A line of meaning. When one person falls out of the conversation, what happens to the words?

Aaron and I had a private language. We had words such as naganunchkee, eliungenser, rabahunee. Saying these words was like flying. In the quiet of the night, back and forth, through the wall, our words would fly.

Nuchkeenamunee! The small intimate voice. Moving into sleep. Moving out of sleep. Words were our song.

I've been away from your voice for so long and the dust keeps settling every day. Recently, when I say nitrous oxide, I say it as if it were an impersonal gas. Like oxygen, for example. To follow the nuances of your death, I have stopped all other work. This is dangerous. I know that.

If it would help, I would cut off my hands and feet, I would remove my breasts. I am aware that these words represent a form of madness. My fingers are long like the branches of a wintering tree. One night at a party, as I spoke to Maggie, you suddenly exclaimed, "Your hands! They are beautiful!" For this reason alone I do not not cut them off.

The house on Partington Ridge, yours and Maggie's, burnt down. In the first weeks after you died, in spite of all warning, I went up there to Big Sur and to L.A. in search of your adulthood. I was undaunted. Inconsolable. My grief set out from each night's dream, and during the long afternoons the insects took it up, sawing the invisible air around me.

The interviews with your friends were useless. No one could tell me what I wanted to know. There was infighting about who had been closest to you. Maggie had stated it simply. "Aaron loved his sister best. He never stopped raving about her large breasts and long legs."

The geography of grief. In our family Los Angeles equals death. But this thinking leaves so few places one can go. It is said that a Jew gains historical context through his or her own personal grief. In this way, I move into history.

You had asked me to watch over your things. The list is finite. A small wooden jar, made in Big Sur by a carpenter with large hands and a kind face. A gold ring with a red stone. Origin unknown. Two sweaters, both in shades of brown, variations on your hair. One quilt made of red velvet with a satin inner side, created by Maggie in a productive phase. Your journals. This is what there is of your life.

Maggie had very small breasts and a sensational ass. A boyish figure or a young girl's body. She smoked Camels. She drank San Miguel beer. One bottle after another. She played the electric violin. She made quilts. She ran the horse farm. She waited on tables. She waited and waited on tables. You wrote once, "I'm dependent on Maggie's dependency." You also wrote in your journal a vivid account of making love with Maggie. You described her little breasts with their large, dark nipples. You described the arch of her back. I shouldn't have read it, but I couldn't stop. I was fascinated by your description of her breasts. I pretended I was fucking Maggie. She was saying, "I love you Loren. I love you. Suck on my breasts." Then I got scared and banged shut the journal.

There is a blank piece of paper in the middle of your journals. This I particularly keep secret. It has three loose-leaf holes along the side and wide lines, not narrow, down the middle. For years I've wondered why you put it there. But I don't move it and I'm patient. Does this mean I'm living with a ghost?

It took me so long to replace your things with mine. I am afraid that you will reappear and notice that I have moved in on top of you. I now have two typewriters. Yours and mine.

And two voices. One on top of the other. So much for envy. Please forgive me. My search now is how to fit us both in.

Once I saw Aaron racing past me in the L.A. airport. This image returns to me often. In his twenties he was already fast-paced and high-strung, his lean body profiled against sadness. He was rushing to catch a plane for the Sur for Thanksgiving to visit old friends on the Ridge. They were preparing turkey and yams for a returning king. By that time he had leapt into the L.A. cinema world. "The Hollywood Left," an article in *Esquire* was to describe it some years after his death. His friends viewed him with both envy and love equally.

On the verge. Aaron was always on the verge. Occasionally he sent friends money and to Maggie he confidentially revealed he had made a will, which was to leave her enough to support her for the rest of her life. But the will was never found, nor was the deed to the alleged land up on the Sonoma coast.

Years later, when I last visited Maggie, she had been going to computer school. "Aaron promised a lot," she said to me sadly, "but still in the end I had to grow up."

Their pet cockatoo had died that year from a chill. Maggie had forgotten to cover it for one night. Just one night. Still, it outlived Aaron by a decade. Earlier that year the cockatoo, who was named Papaguy, because of his assumed maleness, had laid two small eggs. I keep track. Of all of them.

Then there are the dreams. I have lost track of their number. This does not including the visitations, at the tail end of a dream. Just as I was waking to the realization of his death, I would see his afterimage rise at the foot of my bed. Swift. Like the afterglow of a coastal sunset, the room held a silver, luminous light. Faint but distinct. Who is watching over whose things?

Chapter 9

The miraculous and the tragic continue to run neck and neck, constant companions.

Just the other day, here in California, the Santos appeared again. It has fifteen cracks. The sides are warped. The glue has bubbled. It has been living, if you can call that life, in a closet, for the past fifteen years. It reappeared and was delivered to Doug's door the very week of his open-heart surgery. He will live, without his ticking heart, despite what they viewed when they sawed through his rib. The walls between his heart valves were flapping like sails carelessly bound against a mast.

The Santos will be mended by one of the great American guitar repairmen still alive, who happens to live in California. He is taking great care of the Santos. He only works on it when the humidity falls below 55 percent or at night. He dreams of walking through its inner archways as he once strolled through the mazes of the Alhambra with its tinkling fountains of silver water and scent of lemon air.

The Santos is referred to as "the Feather." The lightest flamenco guitar ever made, at least in the collective memory, it was rediscovered in the Pirate's antique store in the Barrio de Santa Cruz, the ancient Jewish ghetto. The Pirate himself doesn't know how it showed up in his shop, but Victór Lopez, Rafael's older, evil-minded brother, knows the Feather's whole story. He won't tell you though, except if you buy the story from him. And that's no way to get a tale. Bad faith.

What we do know is this. Doug, walking by the Pirate's on a fall day, late in the afternoon, on his way from here to there, spotted the Santos hanging naked in the window. His heart ticked quietly. Upon examining the instrument his first intuition was confirmed. He had in his hand a guitar made by the greatest maker ever to have lived. Its blue label seemed to glow with warmth. The date and name showed clear: SANTOS 1921.

Small as an infant, the guitar was so light it was a feather in the arms. Quietly, without uttering a word to the Pirate, Doug sat down in a darkened corner of the shop. He tuned up the strings to A and formed the A-chord with his left hand and with his right hand he began the opening roll to the *bulerías*. Famous for his galloping *bulerías* stride, his *rasgueado* thundered out through the still air of the shop. The chord rang dry and true. The Pirate stood as still as an antique in the sun. Doug stopped as suddenly as he started.

"¿Cuánto es?" he asked the Pirate in a calm tone of voice.

"Ochenta dolares," answered the Pirate. Eighty dollars.

"Hold this," Doug said, affecting as contained a voice as

he could muster. The racing tick of his heart would surely give him away, he thought.

Doug leapt into a taxi and went straight to the bank. He withdrew eighty dollars and then he did a peculiar but understandable thing. He went to a well-known Gypsy bar in Triana and had a drink. He sat there quietly ticking among the other guitarists, nurturing his secret until he glowed. This was Doug's version of machismo.

Shy and introverted by nature, thin as a stick in body and frail as a kite in health, he did not compete in the *cojones* small talk of a Gypsy bar. But he had his own way of matching ego for ego and this was very much his form, a concept the Spaniards are so fond of honoring.

After what seemed to be a longer time than anyone could wait, Doug finished his wine and nodded goodbye to his friends. He walked casually down the street and when he was safely out of sight, he leapt back into a taxi and sped to the Pirate's.

It was still there. He wrapped it in a towel and left the shop with the Feather under his arm.

It is said that Diego loved the Feather best. I don't doubt this knowledgeable hearsay, though the decade that I lived in Morón it was Mary's Reyes he asked for and took to his breast, whenever the feeling of *duende* was thick in the room.

"¿Mary, dónde está la Campaña?" he would say, "Where is the Bell?"

The Reyes was called the Bell because one could hear the bells of the Torre de Oro ringing through its archways. I once told Manuel that if I ever found a man whose hair smelled like the inside of Mary's guitar, I would follow him to the Rock of Gibraltar.

As I had followed his older brother, Ángel, down the coast of Spain from Torremolinos to Algeciras searching for a bed. It is as if our unspent passion that night was put into the Rock, that's how I see it over and over in my mind. Regardless of the scale I am imagining, the Rock comes forth burning red on a blue sea. The Rock comes forth over and over like Monet's haystacks in various shades of pastels over green seas. But when I imagine myself playing the *rondeña* tuned to the key of D minor, the Rock comes forth burning red on this blue sea. The rising sun indistinguishable from the Rock's face.

"Let me live on the face of this rock, burning red," I whispered to Ángel.

"¿Qué, niña?" he groaned in his sleep, throwing a sweating leg over my naked thigh.

I have secretly translated *la rondeña* as the song of longing. I tell this to no one. I could defend the claim as a translator's leaping prerogative. If Ansonini can liken the four corners of his *pañuelo*, his handkerchief, to the four corners of the world; if he can say that Luis's hands broke through the *duende* barrier at the fiesta in Ronda — then, I say that *la rondeña* is the song of longing. And the morning Ángel and I arrived in Algeciras too exhausted to make love, the Great Rock came forth burning red on a blue sea, its face indistinguishable from the rising sun.

Chapter 10

I woke up this morning and examined my fingernails. I noticed that my middle fingernail was rough and uneven. I thought to file it in the particular shape fitting for the flamenco guitar. I am always keeping my fingernails in a state of readiness, even when I have not been playing the guitar. I guess I am not alone in this delusion. My friend Ernesto, or Ernie, as he is called in New York, not only keeps his fingernails filed, but before a flamenco concert he actually puts his playing fingernails on, though he hasn't played for at least ten years.

Putting on your playing nails is no small ritual. And as with all things concerning the *arte,* there is debate, there is disagreement. When I first arrived in Morón, Crazy Glue had just hit, and had completely taken over all other formats, at least with the younger generation, with Diego's nephews. The word for Crazy Glue in Spanish is *pegamento,* and this is what you would see in small, slender tubes lying around on the barroom tables.

The nails on the right hand need reinforcing. The acrobatics of the technique, the rigorous nature of the workout, requires it. Don't jump to conclusions and liken this aid to a microphone. It is nothing of the kind. Any guitarist worth his salt can play without its help. But facing a long day at the bar, and a possible fiesta where playing could last ten hours at a stretch, it's best to be prepared.

First, toilet paper is to found. Which is not always easy in a small town in Spain, and in Bar Pepe was a rarity indeed. A small amount for each of the five nails is portioned off. Perhaps a quarter of a square per nail. This quarter is then bunched up and placed over the tip of the nail. And now the delicate maneuver. The crazy glue is carefully opened, and squirted over the toilet paper that rests on the nail. One blows hard to dry it as fast as possible. With luck, no foreign matter — a stray piece of garlic, for example — lands during the drying.

There were two drawbacks to Crazy Glue that eventually put it in its place among the other methods — women's false nails or cement. The first and most serious was that it tended to rot the real nail underneath. Once this process begins, trouble sets in. Secondly, Crazy Glue is one of the strongest substances known to man. On television, they would show how you could lift a car with one drop of Crazy Glue attached to a crane. In my first attempt my two middle fingers stuck together for days. Everyone had an opinion about how to unstick them, but nothing worked short of giving it time. As with all new crazes in the modern world, this one should have been viewed with the necessary skepticism, but as I said, Crazy Glue hit Morón like a ton of bricks.

Often on a dull afternoon in Bar Pepe, you could find a student or one of the nephews putting on the nails. The act itself, and the concentration necessary for even an adequate job, seemed to draw people to the table to chat with the guitarist. There is something restful in sitting near to another hard at work. Like watching someone paint a fence.

With my hand tremor, I had particular problems with putting on nails. Because of this, I would invariably get glue and toilet paper all over my hands at a table full of laughing Gypsies. At the height of our passion, Manuel would put on my nails for me, right in front of everyone. This was one of the kindest acts I can remember.

Often Diego would conduct an *uñas* (fingernail) inspection, by surprise. On the right hand he would run his finger over the edge of the nail to check for tiny cracks or crevices that would catch on the strings. On the left, he would check each finger for the strength of the callus. There was no way to hide the amount you practiced. It always showed up on the callus. I have seen a guitarist's left-hand fingertips bleed after a long fiesta, if he had gone too long without practicing. Diego would rub his callused fingers over yours and nod knowingly. It occurs to me only now that his fingers were so callused that he couldn't possibly have known if ours were. But we believed he knew.

Even without practice, I still have an adequate callus on my right-hand thumb. Now Rafael feels it whenever we see each other, which is often. Now he nods knowingly. He says, "Toca más, Lorea. Toca más. ¿Un poco, cada día, eh?" Play more, Loren. A little every day.

It's crazy, but I've begun to play scales again. These old aching hands are crawling crablike across the strings. And why not? The world needs mediocre guitarists. It's we who appreciate genius.

It's funny the way the hand begins to move. Just three years ago, it seemed the guitar was lost to me forever, like Manuel, like my childhood. I don't know if this dramatic reversal, this turn toward bitterness, this falling out of grace — out of *compás*, if you will — if this occurs in other passions. I've heard stories enough of the disenchanted. I never shun these people. It would be the same as shunning myself. For there is a part of me always ready to fall out of *compás*. I fall in and out daily.

Yesterday I took my guitar out of its case. I held it in its normal playing position, and I realized in this holding that it was an embrace. The guitar fits into the body the way one fits into a familiar lover, the way lovers lie like spoons curled around each other in bed. This is how easily the guitar moved again into my contours. It bears no grudges. It offers its aroma, its sex, without resistance. I breathed the air inside my guitar and moved into the night-blooming jasmine I first smelled in Lebrija.

The finest siesta I ever had took place in the Pensión Antigua in downtown Lebrija, though all conditions pointed, at best, to a light, broken snooze.

"All colors go together. Just remember that," Mica had once said to me. But had you been in Lebrija that morning, you would have been hard put to remember this wise axiom. Each wall in the small room was covered by a different flowered wallpaper. The halls between the rooms were a color green that created the effect of long afternoons under a large, generous juniper. I fell into a deep sleep despite the whirling paisley patterns of wallpaper clashing in discord at the corners, against the backdrop of the green, still afternoon that I knew was advancing in the halls. And what normal person wouldn't have?

You may have noticed a degree of defensiveness in my question. This will always be the case when it comes to the question of sleep around Katerina. She is in this regard like a child who resists to the last minute "going down" for fear of missing something. "Do we have to do this every day forever?"

"Do what?" I asked Katerina.

"Go to bed."

"Yes," I said. "It's a basic law of existence. Like gravity. Good night now."

But with Katerina, putting off "going down" often meant breaking this basic law. An accomplished napper, Katerina could go without nighttime sleep. And this particular morning we had not slept for two dusty days in pursuit of the *Cante*. The basic law was wreaking its revenge.

There are two pensions in Lebrija. One lies on the outskirts, three minutes from downtown. This is the modern pension. Its main draw is a large, night-blooming jasmine tree in the center of its courtyard. In order to gain the greatest benefit from this loveliest of trees, one had to sleep all afternoon, which in the summer in Lebrija is not difficult. The tree sent its perfume into the night air only after midnight. Its blossoms looked like the ruffles on a *gitana* skirt.

The air is sweet throughout the entire pension. All night people sit quietly under its branches, which have a cooling effect. The rooms of the pension are clean and modern. Beds hard. Floors swept. Walls white with perhaps one picture of the Lord Jesus, and a vase of flowers on a small table. I would sleep there forever, I thought. But no such luck.

Katerina, who had accompanied me on my first trip to Lebrija, had insisted that we move on to the pension which was *más antigua.* Located smack in the middle of town, the Pensión Antigua appeared from the outside to be a ramshackle arbitrary grouping of small crooked structures connected by halls. As we walked in the front door, we were greeted by the nods of several elderly women dressed in black, rocking in chairs. Why do they rest here? I thought. The hallway was narrow and I had to step over feet and legs to move to the back room. The color green advanced in front of me. Katerina smiled contentedly. "Now she's happy," I thought sarcastically. I was desperate for sleep.

I must have been down for not more than an hour when I began to emerge from the depth with a sense of suffocation. Almost at the surface, I awoke with a start and looked around me. I noticed that the wallpaper was still writhing but that this was not the problem. The problem was that what I had believed to be an ordinary window was not. This window opened to the inside. I stood up, weak from the heat and the still, stifling air. I looked through the window and observed another enclosed room housing another panting, sweating napper midway through her siesta. It was Katerina. Oblivious. Again, no windows to the outside.

"Por dios," I muttered as I tumbled out of my room, down a few stairs and into the green halls. Much had changed from when I had stumbled in from the outside just an hour ago.

Now there were at least six rocking, female figures along both sides of the walls in the darkened and wonderfully cool hallway. Way off, at what seemed to be a great distance, was a small rectangular shape of blinding white light. It was the door to the outside. One of the women nodded me toward an empty chair. It was a straight-back, but never mind, I sat down and almost immediately fell into a trance, as close to sleep as possible while still awake. In and out. In and out I fell. I was rocking in and out of sleep on that straight-backed chair. We were all, the six señoritas and I, nodding in and out with an almost imperceptible but much appreciated breeze coming through the rectangle, which was also rocking.

Suddenly the bull appeared. Massive in the doorway. Just as suddenly gone. And then again another. Then there were hundreds of people running past our rectangle of light. Legs and arms. Shouts and cries. The old women winked and nodded at me, and pointed toward the door.

I was napping my way through the annual run of the bulls. No matter. Here in the darkened hall, the imagined and the real bulls ran; timeless as the sighs and heaves of the sleepers, as the soothing green continued its advance along the walls.

I think one could say that a good nap is hard to come by in America, where it has to be stolen from the day. Whereas in Spain, a siesta is given with the day. Twice one can go swimming in the clear, deep waters of rest. And during even the busiest of days, one turns inward, back into the quiet. Unlike progress which moves forward, rest moves backward in time. A culture afraid of death cannot hope for an experience of rest.

A siesta alone, or a siesta with a lover, both are good. All my lovers have had this one quality in common, their ability to take a good nap. Manuel, however, is the champion napper, winning hands-down over the others. He can take two naps in a day. No problem. And when I'm with him, I also, driven as I am, can average two a day. If, of course, a day is to be counted as twenty-four hours.

I am waiting for Manuel's arrival at the *estación de autobuses*. This in itself is something I enjoy, something I look forward to. But before I go to the station, the day's heat has to be gotten through, with its heavy drawn curtains, sweating siesta, the petty haggling at market, and the customary visit and *copa* with Katerina. Then I can begin to get ready to take the bus to the bus station. No rush. He won't be coming until after the heat. *A las ocho.*

It is five in the afternoon. Katerina's apartment still holds an oven of air to contend with. Manuel's body has stayed with me all day. The pressure of his chest. My face is still wet from his sweat, and the thought of him brings wavelike spasms up through my legs. Brushing my teeth, I suddenly hold onto the sink to keep from falling. I sponge bathe in the small bathroom and lie naked on the tile floor to cool down.

Through the window I watch the last edge of afternoon's gold light move down the wall of the building across the street. It turns the whitewash to rose.

Noises of the street rise in late afternoon, as does the heat, to the top of these old apartment buildings. The voices of children's games, arguing old women, and the silence of men coming home from work rise to me. The tiles feel cool against my naked body. Finally I rise as the church bells ring six times. There is still much to be done.

My orange cotton skirt and faded silk blouse. Faded. All faded. I have washed them so many mornings here and hung them to dry on the rooftop. Hung them to scorch in the midday heat until the colors, once vital, are dim against my dark tanned skin. They hang now newly ironed. And I approach them as if for the first time. Every trip produces its own uniform, and for this one — the summer I was thirty and fell in love with Manuel for the second time — it is this skirt and blouse.

I step into the skirt and zip it up the side. It hangs down to the hip bones. I have lost weight though I eat continuously. It must be this sweating. Next I slip the silk blouse over my head. No buttons and a V-neck. I turn toward the mirror and begin to brush my long hair into combs. It will be the last of my trips here with long hair. The combs will lay discarded in a box. But I don't know this yet. I don't know that this is an ending. In fact it seems to me that I have just begun again. With Manuel.

I tuck my money in my bra as Manuel has continually warned me of purse snatching in Sevilla. Okay, I tell him.

Okay, I'll be careful — and I show him the hiding place. He doesn't understand that I grew up in New York City. And I'm glad that he doesn't.

I swing down five flights of stairs and step out into the street. The heat has broken, but its memory is on every face. The strain. It is a busy time on the streets and I walk hugging the building on the shady side, an old habit picked up from the women in black. To avoid the heat, I hop on a bus and am on my way to the station. I already know what the evening will be and I am not bored by this knowing. Instead, a sense of relief, as if I'm being held by the repetition itself. Perhaps the evening will hold one or two *falsetas* — original variations on habitual moves — and that is good enough. I am already looking forward to the chicken Manuel will cook, to the nap we will take, and to the late evening stroll. "But for how long?" my American friends ask me. "How many evenings will you be satisfied with this?"

"I'm not counting," I reply.

I arrive at the bus station fresh, cool, and faded, *a las ocho menos quinze.* I watch the old, dusty buses roll in and the corner bars fill with the greetings of dusty, hot people cooling off. Here in southern Spain, *todo el mundo,* all the world, still takes buses and so the stations resemble market places, teeming with life. From this congestion emerges Manuel. The slightly bald head, characteristic stoop, and kind face is coming toward me. "Hola, guapa," he says, putting his arm through mine, and we're off to the bar.

We walk back to Katerina's apartment which in part will justify the second siesta later that evening, if in fact it needs justification. It is a long walk, but we stop at several bars, me drinking *agua mineral con gas,* and he drinking *cervezitas.* And so the distance is covered with complete ease. Manuel says good evening to many people, which tells you he is from a small pueblo. His manners are quaint and endearing. We stop to buy a chicken whose merits he discusses with the owner. We stop to help a boy with a package cross the street. We stop to look at an old building or to watch a bird, and finally we arrive home, where we stop for the evening meal.

Fixing dinner alone, with Manuel, could be an entire evening. As soon as we enter the apartment, still close and hot from the day's heat, the shirt comes off and the apron goes on. I have never tired of watching Manuel's hands cut vegetables — onions, peppers, tomatoes, garlic. Nor of watching him watch the pot as it cooks. He could wait forever, it seems, adding a bit of saffron here and pepper there. Breathing quietly through his nose, tending the fire, so to speak. As I watch him watch, he gives me my daily Spanish lesson. Going over all the utensils and spices and reviewing other delicacies he had concocted. It is not a time of heated conversation. A light exchange of knowledge to keep the surface of the mind busy, leaving the rest free to attend to the food. It is never the same twice. These one-pot wonders, mixed with saffron rice and always a separate potato tortilla. A small side dish of tomatoes lightly salted with chips of fresh garlic and a dab of oil and vinegar. Bread. And it's ready to serve. On the table it seems a feast.

At the table the reviewing of daily events, their reenactments in caricature, and their philosophical implications occur. Lively and animated, we inhale the food. Always, eating more than is humanly possible is an excellent prelude to a second siesta. "Come más, Lorea," Manuel encourages. Eat more.

He has a theory that my blood is too thin. And this because I drink too much water and not enough beer. When neither of us can eat one more bite of bread soaked in oil and garlic, the drowsiness sets in and so too the *jinilea*. A Gypsy word left over from the ancient tongue of Caló, *jinilea* means the silliness of children before sleep. This wondrous silliness always lies dormant in Manuel's personality, waiting for a moment to emerge in all its glory.

We lie in bed making huge shadow pictures of rabbits against the wall with our hands. The two rabbits, shy of each other, finally, after extensive courting, meet and fall madly in love, stroking each other's ears.

"¿Estás contenta?" Manuel asks. Are you happy?

"Muy," I reply, trying hard not to pronounce it like the "oye" of my Jewish roots.

"¿Estás cansada?" asks Manuel, who has eaten even more than me. "Are you tired?"

"Un poco," I reply, wanting always more *jinilea*.

But Manuel is falling into sleep, holding my sweating body as he sings in a whisper, straight into my ear, a verse about the Torre de Oro we passed by on our walk. His feet against the wall tap out the *compás*.

I slip out of the embrace and move to my small writing table. I will simultaneously write a letter to Mica and watch Manuel sleep. Watching over another's sleep is so private an experience that it is rarely described. It is in itself restful.

And the sleeper feels the watching as if held in a kind of safety only fully believed in childhood.

"Let others roam the globe for *falsetas*," I write to Mica. "I learn my *compás* in the arms of sleep."

By midnight we rise again. We dress quietly, asking after each other's rest. We enter the nightly promenade from bar to bar to meet our friends, refreshed and ready to take on the night, its stories and its songs, filled with the sounds of the crickets, the howling cats, the echoing small plazas, the close stars, and the bars alive with wakened sleepers — all over Sevilla.

A good dose of *cante jondo* in the morning far exceeds even the best *café con leche*. I can't recommend it highly enough. It provides the perfect bridge between the sleeping and waking states. Building a bridge out of the unconscious into the world at large is no small matter. It should be examined with seriousness.

Cante jondo flies straight out of sleep into the world without a glance backward. Out of the cradle into the void it flies, dripping with imagery picked up by that deep current, pulsing with raw rhythm it arrives uncensored, *por derecho,* straight on, as if to defy the morning's workaday concerns. You will lose nothing of your dreams if you ride the *Cante* into the morning. Take heart! Courage is the key. It all fits into one world, and the morning errands can still be done in the afternoon.

I play my tapes on an old, steel Sony that belonged to my brother. This gives a clearer sound than many of the machines I have heard over the years. The cause of that familiar background static indigenous to these tapes may be the result of initially bad recording, with cheap tapes and a hidden microphone, or the equally poor machine that the tapes are replayed on. Most flamenco tapes create the illusion that the music is forever receding into dust almost at the instant one hears the clear note ring true.

Many have made the mistake of buying the best tape machines before going to Spain, in an attempt to deal with the source problem. Thousands of dollars have been spent on the newest, smallest, most technologically advanced recorders. These invariably break when they arrive in Andalusia. Perhaps it is the dust. Suddenly the start button won't work. One thing's for sure. There's not a shop in Sevilla that can fix a sophisticated Japanese machine.

Manuel's tape recorder is made of plastic. Black, with red push-buttons, it lives next to his bed on a small table along with one glass barroom ashtray filled with day-old, week-old, year-old cigarette butts. Winstons. A *tinto* glass or two. And scattered tapes that range from a Diego fiesta (1951) to a store-bought tape of Antonio Mairena, a Paco de Lucía tape, and possibly even a tasteless popular singer of Latin love songs. This covers the whole range of Manuel's landscape. One foot in the preindustrial world. One foot in the modern.

Manuel rolls over in bed. It might be five in the afternoon or five in the morning. He pushes a red button with an arrow pointing forward and out pops Diego's *toque*. His *soleares* shimmers. The initiating *falseta* is a singular statement.

What comes next is a motor scooter revving up its engine. This tells you that the fiesta must have taken place in a bar. Morning had arrived and the outside world was preparing for work. More street noises. More *soleares*. Static. A racking cough that could only have been Ansonini's morning hack, and then the music stopped as suddenly as it started.

"Niña!" Diego was exclaiming. "Dame agua. ¡A-g-u-a!"

The niña might very well have been the sixty-year-old Fernanda. According to Manuel, the last word Diego uttered before allowing the life to pass from him was *"niña."* We have no way to verify this, but to me, it sounds authentic. "Child" most certainly was one of Diego's core words.

Manuel, who had seemed to be asleep, disengages his leg from mine, rolls over again, and punches the fast-forward button with a groan. This small piece of technology allows us to skip over fifteen minutes or so of boring conversation. In all fairness to the participants, it was probably not boring in the moment. But this taped "moment" of relaxed, post-dawn exchange happened twenty years ago, and if ever there is a situation about which one can say, "You had to be there," surely it is the stream of repetitive chatter that flows like a current in between the pulsing outbursts of music.

Every so often in this current of talk a distinct voice rises with a declaration of great profundity or astonishing banality. I have often wondered what the speaker would think if he or she knew they had been immortalized in this way. That two lovers twenty years later, drifting in and out of sleep in a sagging double bed, were hearing that statement.

"Pepe. Traeme una tapita. Ahora mismo."

Manuel leaves off the fast forward button and moves back to my side of the bed, curling around me. We rock very slightly, two spoons, listening to *bulerías,* the form that bridges the light song and the deep song. *Bulerías* can go light. *Bulerías* can go dark. And, so too, with sensuality.

The conversation before *bulerías* is staccato. From the low hum background noise that a *soleares* produces, the impulse toward the *bulerías* is marked by a sudden pickup in pace. Drinks are ordered. Favorite jokes are pulled out of the bag. Clinking of glasses. Laughter. You can feel it building. An almost physical longing for its rolling twelve beats and bouncing sixes endures, even after twenty years. Everyone strains toward the form. The guitarist tunes up the A-chord. It will be a *bulerías,* we all hope. We will give birth to the *bulerías.* The tuning up goes on longer than any of us can bear. More drinks. More tuning of that one A-chord. There is a slight possibility that the form will be out of tune with his listeners' longing. That the guitarist will launch into a *soleá* in A instead. I have heard it happen many times. And in one minute the music is dead and the room becomes flat and lifeless. But this is a Diego tape. And Diego never misses. That was his genius. He had the pulse. His ear was attuned to the longing around him. And that longing translated directly into his thumb. Down it goes onto the A-chord and we're off.

I catch a phrase of a *letra* and poke Manuel in the ribs. "Wake up. Wake up, Manuel. ¿Qué dice el cantaor?" What is the singer saying?

"Tu entiendes," Manuel stammers. You understand.

In my own defense, I believe you would have to live with a Gypsy for no less than ten years to pick up a passing *bulerías* verse off a bad tape, recorded on a worse machine. "No, No," I say with increasing urgency. I climb over Manuel and press the rewind button and then the start button in quick, adept movements. I've been through this many times before. "Manuel. Manuel." I whisper in his ear. "Por favor. ¿Qué dice el cantaor?"

"Dice esto," Manuel whispers back.

> Ay qué con los ojos seña
> en algunos ocasiones
> los ojos sirven de leña.

When Manuel says it slowly, then I get it.

> Eyes make signals,
> On certain occasions
> Eyes act like firewood.

"¿Qué buena letra!" Manuel says good-naturedly, though he was rudely awakened from deep sleep.

"Qué bien," I agree. It is the essence of the *bulerías*, I muse, as I ride the *Cante* once again backward into sleep.

Chapter 11

I have been packing to leave for Spain again for almost a year. The view in front of my house is a quiet suburban street, lined with cars. Two or three people pass by in an hour, and sometimes several dogs. As I look at my street, I can see a street in Sevilla superimposed. What variety of life! The blind lottery-caller in her thick Andalusian dialect calling, "Ciento sesenta y tres. El premio quedao." This goes on all day. In the neighborhood bars, department stores, laundromats, an overtone or undertone of Spain. By the time I go, I'll have already been there.

Ansonini is a global personality. This man carries his home in his Panama hat. We bought our old Gypsy friend a round-trip ticket to do a Christmas fiesta in Berkeley. The first day there, he met my friend Kate, who claims she was so struck down by love that it was some time before she noticed that he had no teeth. And so he stayed. He is at home standing in a bar in California. He is at home leaning up against a bar in Sevilla. I could never quite decide whether Ansonini was a Zen master or an oblivious old fool. I think that still I am not sure if Ansonini is dead or alive. The other day, down at the marina, I thought I saw his hat flying high above the hill. It was a kite.

Watching Ansonini light a cigarette in an Irish bar in Berkeley appeases my longing. His posture — torso erect, hands like a bird, arms definitive — tells you that he knows he's at home in this moment, with this yellow, afternoon light filtering through the windows. He was born before the great irrevocable change. Before they put the TV in Bar Pepe.

This afternoon a grim, grey-white day stretched out in front of my study window. The sun would not break through, the way it often does here, just as my homesickness for all places and people who have touched me would not quit. I had to abandon my work altogether and head out to Brennan's to see my old friend, Ansonini. There he was, standing at the bar and holding his afternoon court with anyone who happened within his territory. I received enough abrazos, hugs, for ten people and then he launched into a rapid conversation with me that to any outsider would have appeared as if he were yelling at me for some unpardonable sin. Never having mastered even the slightest understanding of his Spanish, which was even harder than Diego's to understand, I listened as Ansonini ranted on, convinced of my absolute understanding.

A rather conservative-looking couple, down the bar, leaned over and asked me in polite and formal English, with a Spanish accent what country Ansonini was from. And what language was he speaking?

"¿Qué dice?" Ansonini howled at me.

"Dice que de dónde es usted," I said in an equally loud voice, as if responding to an accusation.

"De Andalusia," Ansonini said as if stating the obvious and essential at once.

The couple try to mask their absolute surprise as they tell us that they also hail from this province.

"¡Viva tu!" says Ansonini, so confident of his voice that the unintended insult flew over his head, and dissolved in the yellow, afternoon lull of Brennan's bar.

"¡Bebe!" continued Ansonini, as he ordered a round of drinks for these people from his home ground.

They moved towards us, their guard down, and their faces now open to the moment. "Mucho gusto. Mucho gusto." Pleased to meet you, they said over and over as they shook his hand and moved in, under his enormous wing.

Ansonini may be dying. We don't know for sure. We are five thousand miles from the dear old man. And our sources are unreliable to say the least. Had we heard directly from Ansonini, the horse's mouth, still we would be as far from the truth as now. Ansonini lies the way he sings. With force. And they come hand in hand. He may do neither again.

The thought of Ansonini dying is not devastating. Who doesn't anticipate that a seventy-year-old man will die? It's not tragic. It's something else. We're down to the last few. They don't make rocks like him anymore. We were all children together. Even the old ones, though they died sooner. Only the city itself kept aging and, as if to make up for its inhabitants, the walls crumbled before our eyes.

I've been tired for days. And coincidentally, it's been raining for days. If there wasn't a continual parade of umbrellas outside this window, I would despair. The march of umbrellas keeps me on track. And the hats keep a close second.

Manuel and I walked side by side, under one umbrella, in the rain, on the last day of feria, through the streets of Sevilla.

Andamos
debajo de un paraguas
por las calles de Sevilla
en la primavera.

We walk
Under an umbrella
in the streets of Sevilla
in the spring.

This runs the danger of incorrigible romanticism. But if you could see Manuel, you'd know we would be safe from this danger.

Manuel is a balding, overweight, middle-aged Gypsy. He wears polyester pants. In fact, when I showed Mica a picture of Manuel, from my most recent trip, she actually said that Manuel looked like an aging Nazi living in Argentina. In all fairness to Manuel, those pictures in no way captured his essence.

In addition to three pictures of Manuel dressed in grey pants, a grey sweater, and a purple *pañuelo* around his neck, there were sixteen pictures of an identical view from my window. A small room on the rooftop of an ancient building, across the street from the giralda; you could see the rooftops, it seemed, of all Sevilla. The laundry hung like clouds in the stillness of the afternoon. And at night, the moon preferred the giralda to all other steeples. It hung out next to the old clock, the way I hung out in the neighborhood bar. But the light in these pictures was so bad, it made Sevilla look like Brooklyn. Grey and dingy.

Besides, Mica has a long-standing grudge against Manuel. It is rooted in Mica's claim that Manuel ran out on a large bar bill, after a festive dinner gathering in Bar Miguel, in Morón. Jim, Mica's husband, also claims that with Manuel this is a habit. Though I admit that Manuel has often been seen making a back-door exit, he is usually in flight from an advancing fiesta, where the flamenco vultures are sure to follow. I also concede that Manuel is not at all above walking out on a bar bill, but still he has dignity — of a certain and pronounced kind.

They all have dignity. The uncle Diego, Ansonini, Manuel, Rafael, Fernanda. I could go on. It is possible that Diego set the tone, but the form of dignity seems to me to be quite old. It is a form of greeting, recognizable by others attuned to the same voice.

Take, for example, the story of Diego and the silk *pañuelos*. As a gift, a rich señorita gave Diego six silk *pañuelos*. There were times on summer evenings when the rich folks of Morón would go slumming. They would tumble into Bar Pepe with a pocket full of coins. The music on nights like this was competent, but not *jondo*. In any case, a certain señorita was moved to give Diego *pañuelos*. A gift not only of great monetary value, but also a gift with implications.

The next day Diego and friends, including Ansonini, went to the river to cook up a paella and to relax from the night's work. Diego disappeared into the woods with his box of *pañuelos*. Ansonini followed shortly after. Hanging from the tree branches, scattered about, were six soiled silk *pañuelos*. "Diego," Ansonini howled, "¿Qué pasó con tus pañuelos bonitos?" What happened to your beautiful hankerchiefs? Diego smiled and pointed to his rear.

Chapter 12

The relationship between music and optimism is not a casual one. The chord resolves. A to B-flat to A.

During my lesson today, Doug told me the story of Manolo de Huelva, one of the greatest of all flamenco guitarists. At the end of his life he was a bitter man, hurling warnings at all would-be guitarists about the degenerate condition of the art of flamenco. His whole life was a raging battle against discovery. He played behind doors and only to his wife. And yet his reputation grew. Doug got it in mind to hear Manolo play. He moved into an apartment that was under Manolo's and was above an old bar in Madrid. He spent days, weeks, months sitting on the stairwell listening to the muted sounds seep through the cracks in the door. Finally one day Doug offered Manolo a huge sum of money to play at a fiesta. Manolo accepted on the grounds that there would be no tape machine present. Doug assured him and then he sneaked his machine into the fiesta and he recorded. In the end, Doug, having been found out, pretended to erase the material, but did not. Manolo was too unsophisticated to understand and he left satisfied.

Today, during my lesson, I heard this tape. "His *siguiriyas* is so dry," Doug said, "that it only has one *falseta*. He goes completely silent on the 11th and 12th beats." The chord resolves. A to B-flat to A. The singer sings a verse from 1909:

> Tus ventanas oyen mis penas
> como oyen mis alegrías
> ¿cuántos secretos guardan
> las ventanas de Andalusia?

> Your windows hear my pain
> Your windows hear my happiness
> How many secrets are guarded
> By the windows of Andalusia?

I keep taking my house apart and putting it back together again. I am becoming an expert at this going and coming. Over and over again, I pack but I don't leave. Mica is right. I have a strange obsession with her photographs. They are all over my house. In this one, Mica is standing on a dirt floor in an adobe hut. The doors and the windows are open. Light is streaming in through the open door and window. You can't tell if it's ocean or desert out there.

Mica wears a bandana around her head. A man's V-neck sweater and her shirt hanging out of her pants. She is barefoot and the ring on her second toe is visible. This is a baffling ornament. And knowing Mica now for seven years has not aided in explanation. Why does she wear this silver toe ring? Day after day? She who is otherwise modest and handles her exotic beauty with such caution.

In truth, Mica looks like a Peruvian Miss America. When I first met her in Berkeley, she exclaimed, "Are you the Loren who lived three doors up from Bar Pepe?"

Stunned I replied, "Yes I am, but how do you know?"

"Your place," she explained, "was called 'Loren's place,' and whoever arrived from America lived there to carry on the tradition after being blessed by Ansonini, who used to say, "You must know Loren, she lives in the United States."

In this snapshot Mica seems to have been up all night, her usual understated style is completely submerged by the man's sweater. There are several empty wooden chairs strewn about the dirt floor, which makes one suspect there had been a fiesta the night before.

Mica looks up at the camera cockeyed with a bandana on her head. The light of the desert or the ocean, I don't know which, is flooding the picture. I keep cleaning the dirt from the floor off the frame.

At this moment, two pictures of dear old Ansonini are sliding out of my writing journal. There were so many pictures of him that choosing one is almost arbitrary. But nonetheless, I chose the one of him singing to a wreath of garlic, which he is embracing in his hands. He is wearing his famous turquoise shirt, a red *pañuelo* around the neck, grey sideburns, and he has an expression on his face one sees on a new lover's face at the start of a wild flirtation.

Ansonini was past seventy when he died yesterday morning in Morón. That his right hand had been paralyzed and that he couldn't walk did not, I am told, stop the neighborhood bar from reviving the best Bar Pepe days. Old and young Gypsy artists appeared night after night in the sweltering heat to sing and dance for Ansonini. Like some prehistoric bird, this man's wing was so large it could shelter men eighty years old, raging adolescents, children, blossoming young girls, and bitter, middle-aged women.

Last night we gathered at Kate's old house in Berkeley and sat around a table full of pictures. I just kept holding Mica's hand. They're taking Ansonini to Puerto this morning. The town of his birth, hundreds of miles from Sevilla. Mica leans over and whispers in my ear:

"They'll bury him in his empty suitcase yet!"

I can depend on Mica to be irreverent and this is why I hold her hand. It's not a large hand like mine. She is slight by nature though one rarely notices this because her character is so strong. My hand in hers is twice the size, though her hand is the comforter. I place my hand and hers under her thigh. She leaves her hand there with mine.

"They'll bury him in a cardboard suitcase in Puerto," I say, "where no one knows him."

We laugh.

The full moon will always remind me of Sevilla. The city itself is the incorrigible romantic. The inhabitants are more secondary than they would like to believe.

It is August. And the hills are various shades of brown. I am aware of a similarity in landscape. In Andalusia, in

August, the hills are scorched white, one step beyond brown. It seems I have never noticed the beauty of northern California, but all these years this beauty has been accumulating. The dry hills, the brown grasses, the bare mountains; these I love as if other forms of beauty were too rich. Especially today. I know that I am avoiding the topic of Ansonini. But here's a secret: For me, Ansonini is not dead.

Mica told me that when they buried Diego they forgot to take his shoes off, and his feet, with shoes on, stuck out of the horizontal grave. Or did I dream this detail? Often I'm tempted to call her up and ask her:

"Mica, by the way, did you tell me that Diego was buried with his shoes on?" And now, to make matters worse, I have become convinced that Ansonini will be buried in his empty cardboard suitcase. Oh, Mica!

In Puerto, no one knows Ansonini. This is the town of his name: Ansonini del Puerto. The reason I know that no one knows Ansonini in the town of his name is not because Ansonini told me that. Quite the opposite. According to Ansonini, the original forked tongue, everyone knew him in Puerto. None of us would have been the wiser, if Ansonini hadn't insisted on retrieving his suitcases from Puerto.

When I received a letter from Manuel proposing the trip, with his handwriting slanting down, and all his thoughts rushing into one long sentence with a period at the end of the page, my year of packing was over and I was ready to go. I explained to my friends, "We have important business in Puerto."

The past keeps accumulating at an alarming rate, but this never seemed to hurry the progression of our journey. Nothing ever does hurry the anticipation or the development of *gusto*. To be *a gusto* is its own achievement in any given day. To be with others *a gusto* is deserving of at least a song. The best translation I can arrive at for group *gusto* is present happiness. Mica has said many times that nowhere has she laughed harder than in Spain. The kind of laughing that causes dry heaves, hiccoughs, tears, and other maladies. *Gusto* has something to do with valuing time in itself as it passes.

The morning we departed from the Bar Pepe — Jim, Mica, Katerina, Ansonini and I — we did, in fact, have a plan. Ansonini was in true form. Still in his three-tooth epoch, one could almost say he was a young man. Except for the fact that he wasn't. Of course no one ever knew his real age, but let's hazard a guess in the mid-fifties. Or put it this way. He was old enough to have left three-quarters of his life in another place where no one who now knew him had ever been.

How Ansonini, the only blue-eyed Gypsy I ever knew, first arrived in Morón is a story whose lineage I have never successfully traced. It seemed he had always been there, yet there were frequent references to Puerto. The town where everybody knew him. The town of his birth. And the town where, whatever he lacked in Morón, whether it be a razor, a favorite *pañuelo*, or a *camisa,* was invariably left in his suitcases, which were left in Puerto. That it was the town where Ansonini had married and lived for forty years is true. Also true is his grave in the quiet, lovely cemetery in Puerto. The rest, however, is up for grabs.

The plan was simple and straightforward. In Jim's van, we would drive to Puerto. A three- to four-hour drive to the sea. There, we would drink at the bar where everyone knew him, and have a lavish dinner at his favorite restaurant, whose chef would create a feast in honor of his return. After that, a stroll through the town and then we'd pick up the suitcases at the pension where he had lived and then back to Morón.

Returning to one's roots is never without its hazards. This much we all know. But somehow the particular nature of the hazard eludes us, as does a dream, until we are definitively within its grips. The idea of retrieving that which is lost apparently flows eternal in the human soul.

But on the morning of our trip, although all of us were old enough to know better, none of us did. The tone was jubilant. We walked en masse to Bar Pepe to pick up Ansonini and although the town clock struck only eleven in the morning our friend was already *a gusto* on cognac and on the day. And so it was much to everyone's surprise that fifteen minutes past the old white cement factory on the edge of town, Ansonini implored Katerina to stop at the first *venta*. The cheese, he said, was worth its weight in gold. To no one's surprise, however, it was the sherry that was tasted and passed around. And so the trip progressed.

Stopping at every *venta* between Morón and Puerto, what was at most a five-hour drive became a ten-hour journey. A journey of group *gusto*. Driving down the mountain from Ronda, with the sunset a spectacular, salmon-colored red, must have spurred on Ansonini to not only say, but to swear, that a meal of a fifteen-pound fresh salmon was waiting for us in Puerto. He even made a phone call to the proprietor of the bar, or so we thought. All the way down the mountain as the salmon sun dropped into the sea, Ansonini expanded the dinner as if to match the grandness of the view. Perhaps this is the way he spun his magnificent lies, in accordance with the natural beauty around him. And so our appetites increased as we wound our way down the mountain toward Puerto. The imagined dinner became larger at every *venta*.

In all fairness to Ansonini, the proprietor of the bar did, in fact, throw his arms around the old man and real tears brimmed in his eyes, so that over and over he removed his glasses and wiped them clean of steam on his white apron. But no salmon appeared and in fact no seafood was to be had, though the meal was plentiful in its own right. We all pretended that we'd never seen the salmon sun, except for Katerina, who rode him mercilessly. And why shouldn't she? They'd been at each other for over a decade about the Truth. Why stop now?

I couldn't have been more relieved that it was Jim and not Katerina who discovered the truth of the suitcases. There are, after all, certain areas of one's life that are not to be challenged, especially by one's closest friends. I would not have let Ansonini know that I knew the contents of his suitcases were I up against a firing squad. No indeed. Some lies are worth dying for!

By the time we reached the pension where his suitcases had lived undisturbed for fifteen years, it was quite late and the group of us pulling up in the van still had a carnival feel.

We all entered together. The proprietor embraced Ansonini and one by one, we, his young friends, were introduced with great pomp.

Ansonini disappeared into the inner gloom of the pension and Katerina held conversation with the old proprietor. Ansonini's young friends must have appeared like elves to him. He kept looking at us in disbelief. "The old man was old when he left here," he must have thought, "and now fifteen years later, he appears looking younger, minus two teeth, and tailed by a group of adoring youngsters." He clung to Katerina's words to remain oriented.

Ansonini reappeared, bent by the weight of his suitcases, one in each hand. Oh how heavy they seemed! We all but Katerina rushed to his aid.

"No," he hollered. "¡Déjame solo!" Leave me alone!

We backed off as he plopped them down, making the dust fly.

"Gracias, viejo." He embraced the proprietor solemnly.

One thing about Ansonini. He could create a mood. He lifted both suitcases again, slowly and with difficulty.

"¡Ven!" he said to the group of us and out we went. Come!

Ansonini carefully placed his bags into the back of the van. Walking around to the front door, he climbed in and was asleep in minutes.

Pulling up to the Pensión Pasqual, Ansonini's base in Morón, several hours later, just before dawn, we all got out of the car quietly, so as not to wake him. He seemed particularly exhausted. We were all exhausted.

Jim went around to the back of the van to take the bags out and up to Ansonini's room. The others headed for the door. I stayed behind to help Ansonini out of the van. I saw Jim take his balance, bending his knees as he leaned over to carry the great weight of the suitcases. As he grabbed the handles of the bags, I saw them practically fly out of the van over his head, and he himself almost fell over backwards with a look of disbelief on his face.

It was the kind of moment of disbelief that lives outside of time. A moment when the anticipated is suddenly pulled out from under you and you are left face to face with nothing save your own smallness. I caught Jim's eye.

Jim gasped. And then he made a split-second decision. It was an opportunity for true heroism, an opportunitiy that doesn't come often. Before anyone could turn around, Jim's body regained its composure, he bent as if with the weight of the suitcases.

"Boy! Are these heavy!" he exclaimed.

Ansonini had awakened and was already yelling at Jim, as he emerged from the van, "¡Cuidado, niño! Cuidado." Careful, child! Careful.

I am prone to believe that we all carry empty suitcases filled with our past. Ansonini's were simply more concrete, and perhaps to his credit he was able at last to retrieve them and deposit them where they belonged.

I am told that I tried to jump into Aaron's grave as the casket was lowered. I have no memory of this. None. My last memory is of watching Maggie throw a bouquet of Big Sur flowers in over the casket. What kind of word is that? Casket.

I remember riding to Westchester in a car that was black and had a backseat as big as a room. Was the casket with us? I can see my face outside the car looking in. I see a white face pressing up against the window. The face doesn't understand on which coast it has landed. Does the sun rise in the East? Set in the West? Already I have become a refugee within my own life.

I've never seen Aaron's grave again. Not once since they lowered him down into the earth. I didn't believe he was inside that box and I don't believe it now. The moment they lowered Aaron's casket into the ground, I wasn't in my body and he wasn't in his box. I can't tell you exactly where we were, but I can say in a certain way I've been trying to locate myself in time and place ever since that moment of dislocation. That's one word for it. Dislocation. It's one of those words that abstracts experience to give the semblance of control. Like saying: "He passed away." Instead of: "He's dead. Dead as a doorknob."

My parents went to California and dug up a small Torre pine tree for the grave. Instead of a stone. In essence, a nice idea. A healing symbol for them and, who knows, perhaps for Aaron. But as for me, I feel like that dug-up Torre pine every time I go back East. It's like I had been carried to my own grave. It was hit or miss for years whether that tree would survive the East Coast winters, and great importance was placed on its survival. Special forest consultants were brought in to examine it. Would it grow? Would it be a stunted pine? It seemed I remembered the same questions being asked about Aaron when he was little.

I have to think about my own survival now. I can't be worrying about that tree the way my folks do. They go visit Aaron there quite a bit, and always on the "anniversary day." Another strange set of words. The day he married death. They go to visit him less now, but still enough to keep watch. It occurs to me now that they must be watching over his childhood. Because in fact, he never lived on the East Coast after he was seventeen. And if ever there was a happily transplanted spirit, it was Aaron on the West Coast. That's why I prefer to visit him out here. Here he is a sail out on the great blue.

Location, in fact, seems to make no difference whatsoever. I went back to Spain with the idea of visiting Puerto, where Ansonini was buried. I never arrived because in part, for me, Ansonini lived in California. Why? Because that's where I lived when he died. I buried him in my heart in Berkeley, California, where he did not belong any more than my brother Aaron belongs in New York.

When I went back to Spain to visit the grave of Ansonini I never got farther than Sevilla. The stories of Ansonini's death lived there. They were alive and well, like *falsetas*. Stories that go on with no beginning or end. Stories that live whether they are being told or not.

Ansonini arriving home to his wife in Puerto, time after time, deranged at dawn, with no shirt, wearing red underwear on his head as a hat. This lovely image was offered to me by an anonymous aficionado, who was sitting by the open casket with Ansonini's wife, his daughter, and a few others.

"I'd send him out clean and well dressed for a fiesta, and he'd come home at dawn with no shirt, no jacket, and red panties pulled down to his blue eyes with his hair sticking out the leg holes."

No one ever quite believed that Ansonini had a wife. But there she was. Alive as he was dead, a wife of seventeen years, and a daughter with his face. It made us realize how little we had of him, though we had felt we had the whole man and his history. Yet here was seventeen years of his youth in flesh and blood with her own tale to tell. It was part of his gift to make you feel as if nothing in his life existed before he met you.

She offered another astonishing fact. "Ansonini," she said, "had no mother." But there was not a verse that he sang that he did not dedicate to his mother. "Por la gloria de mi madre," he would state, emphatically banging his fist on the table, and then you knew you were in for something good. It was the bedrock of his soul. The core of his *gusto*. According to his wife, Ansonini was raised by a stepmother and his real mother had died in childbirth. I knew that Ansonini spun tales about his life, the way Rumpelstiltskin spun straw into gold. But did Ansonini literally create his own history as he went along? This small but significant discrepancy brought tears to my eyes. I felt outraged when his obituary in ABC stated that Ansonini had been without a mother of his own. "No tenía una madre el mismo." This fact was a lie as big as any he had told. *¡Mentiras! ¡Mentiras!* Lies! Lies!

Ansonini has fallen. Another April will come and go. Another Feria de Sevilla will light up and dissolve into the dust. When I put my mind to this thought I feel a terrible sense of desperation. That modern-day Spain no longer holds the secret power of the *Cante* is a distressing possibility. We have all heard rumors of ruined fiestas, of dishonest *falsetas* being sold in the marketplace, of the *bulerías* being played with thirteen beats instead of twelve. Who will guard the archetypes from these unspeakable violations now that Ansonini is gone? The knowledge of this truth suddenly hits me. I feel the dust from the Feria de Sevilla blowing the eucalyptus leaves down the long road home.

PART THREE

Siguiriyas
Song of Weeping

Chapter 13

Listening to *siguiriyas* this morning, I hear one chord suspended within twelve beats of background rhythm. The other beats are barely audible, like light brush strokes on a canvas. And then one pronounced chord resonates against the background of light brush strokes. The singer's voice, in this case La Fernanda's, is flying out and over the six beats, as if that voice would never return. As if it would fly out through the streets and alleyways of Sevilla, through the darkened churches, the quiet plazas, the noisy flea markets, and finally the long dry road home to Utrera. But no. The voice returns because it hears before we do the anticipation of the next chord that will give the voice a temporary home. It will lure the voice back from its wild flight. It will be the nest for the bird to land and the singer will perceive this in the intake of breath as the guitarist lifts the right hand and moves it down across the B-flat.

This chord alone makes me long to play the guitar. I want to feel the strings moving under my right hand. I want to smell the wood and air inside the body of my Ramírez. I have lent it to Rafael and suddenly I am lonely for it. I am possessive of it. I don't want his hands on my strings. His chin resting where mine has been. I want the guitar to be marked by only me.

I lent my guitar to Rafael because his needed fixing and because mine had not been touched for some years. But this morning I would start all over. Even from scratch. I would once again begin the long road home to the A-chord. I would once again be a beginner in this strange art. The elite art of the decrepit.

To say that I would once again be a beginner is no small matter. To others who have set out along this solitary path, the thought of beginning again would be like being run over by a truckload of drunken Gypsies. Still though, I believe I would embark, even knowing what I do. Knowing that in the end, as far as performance goes, the most I could hope for would be, perhaps, to play background to a fine singer's lesson. This is a compromise of my original dream. I would call it the dream of my youth had it not extended so far into my adulthood. The fantasy is always the same.

I walk into a small neighborhood bar. Perhaps in Morón. No. Not in Morón. Even in fantasy I can not draw my attention away from the nephews. If they labored in the shadow of Diego, I labored in the shadow of their shadows. No. It would not be Morón. Nor Utrera. More anonymous. A bar in Triana would do fine. A small bar smelling of meat and garlic. Late evening. No. Early morning. La madrugada. Dawn. We are ragged with fatigue. There would be Ansonini, one or two interchangeable aficionados, a Gypsy guitarist with a broken thumbnail, and me.

Stopping in for a nightcap or a morning coffee after a night of *cachondeo,* some childlike fun, the *gusto* level high, Ansonini would begin to rap his knuckles on the bar, at first absent-mindedly, and then with more force. A signal as sure as hearing hoofbeats in the distance and then closer, just around the corner. Eyes turning toward Pedro, the male Gypsy guitarist, and he would say: "¡Hombre! ¡No puedo! Verdad. Lo juro. La uña está rota. Lo siento." Friend, I can't play. I swear it. My fingernail is broken. I am sorry.

Then it would begin. A long, boring, soliloquy on how, when, and why it broke, and the serious consequences he and his family are facing as a result. "Verdad. No puedo tocar aquí porque mañana hay un festival." Truly. I cannot play. Tomorrow I have to work at a festival and I have to be prepared.

False sympathetic nods. Hoofbeats continue. Coming closer, just out of sight. The aficionados have no pity on the broken nail. They don't care. Break every nail and still they won't care. What matters is the need for an A-chord, terse and dry, to break into the hoofbeats. This need becomes physical. Ansonini suddenly turns towards me. Almost an after-thought. "Lorea," he would say, quietly for him. "Toca. Pedro. Préstate la guitarra a Lorea. Ella toca bastante bien." Loren, play. Pedro, lend her your guitar. She plays well enough.

"¡Toca!" is what Ansonini said to me the day he first told me about the white raven.

"¡Toca!" he howled as his cognac glass crashed against the round oak table and he reached for the wood tray he was using for a *tabla,* because he had no wooden Andalusian bar here in California. We were as far from the bar of my dreams as a dream can go and still remain potent. We were not in Triana by any stretch, but in Kate's house and I had been hired to play guitar for a solo dance lesson. My first job. Nothing to write home about. But for me, a thrill. The dancer asked for me.

The first time I knew ambition for what it is, its raw power, was this day I accompanied Ansonini with the dancer. It was a shock to discover the extent of my ambition and the way it drove me. Was this the end of childhood? I wanted to accompany his song. Only his. One person. One form. One song. I wanted to learn to accompany age.

I dressed down for the occasion. Not even a comb in my hair. I wanted to be low-profile. I thought this would quiet the nerves that were building with ferocity. To my surprise, when I knocked on the door, Doug answered. He was visiting Ansonini.

Surprises and nervous people don't blend. I attempted an *abrazo,* but it was hollow, cold. Doug smiled and ticked. That helped.

"Lorea!" Ansonini growled from the other room. "Ven acá." He and the dancer were sitting at the table smoking and drinking cognac.

"¡Quieres tomar de chorizo, niña?" Ansonini asked. Do you want some sausage?

"Claro," I said. Sure.

Ansonini took me by the arm and dragged me into the kitchen closet to display dozens of homemade garlic sausages hanging like pigs' tails from the ceiling. "Eh, Lorea," he chuckled. "Bien," he muttered gleefully as he chose among the many.

With extraordinary love he fondled the sausage before he expertly sliced several pieces and served them to me.

"¡Come tu!" Eat! Ansonini, I realized, spoke always in the imperative.

I had once brought one of Ansonini's homemade sausages home to my parents. I had wrapped it in several layers of tinfoil and then in thick brown paper. I carried it in a handbag onto the plane. By the time we passed over the Rockies, the whole plane smelled of garlic. Ansonini's chorizos were not for lightweights.

"¡Come!" he encouraged. I downed them like a stiff drink.

When a singer sings for a dance lesson, he or she normally sings *en voz medio*. In a half-voice. Why? Because the full *cante* requires a force of breath behind it at least as powerful as a burro's braying at dawn. There is no reason to put the body through this unless it's for real. We aren't given enough wind in one lifetime to spare it for many false or half-hearted brays.

Ansonini began to rap his knuckles on the table in slow twelve, warming up with a *bulerías por soleá*. A slow, rolling, sexy *compás* with which I was quite intimate. We had practiced this form many times in my own lessons. "Thank God," I thought as he began with the *tabla*. At least, a form I know.

It had been rumored about town that I played a damn good *bulerías*. Not a *falseta* did I know. But my *compás* was pure. It had its own way of entering the bones and as well a catchy little syncopation where you'd least expect. And so, Ansonini moved easily into the *compás* with obvious delight.

I don't know when it happened that he began to lose interest in the dancer, and move into his own song. But it must have coincided with the cessation of my hand tremor as I became more relaxed. I do remember this: It was surprisingly early on.

Suddenly in the middle of the dancer's *vuelta* — her turn — his knuckles stopped. The dancer paused, astonished. "Toca por siguiriyas," he said quietly to me.

I sat directly across from him, both of us in straight-backed chairs, our knees touching. "¿Qué?" I exclaimed in shock. "Tu sabes que yo no puedo tocar por siguiriyas. Nadie me lo enseñó. Tu sabes eso." You know I can't play *siguiriyas*.

"¡Toca siguiriyas!" he howled into my face and with no more discussion his knuckles began to rap out the rocking, slow *compás*.

I began the announcement of the *siguiriyas* on the A-chord. Three rolling *rasgueados* and then a simple statement of the first *compás*. This is it, I thought to myself, remembering a fiesta several years earlier in New York where the American guitarist had arrived, taken one look at Ansonini and fled down the stairs, leaving only me. My hand shook so when I tried to play, even with my back to the audience, the guitar bounced off my knee. Ansonini had patted my head and called me "*niña*."

It's now or never. That moment of intersection between dream and reality was upon me. When a long-standing fantasy is about to fall, the moment comes unannounced and unexpected, though it seems you've been training your whole life. My fingers surprised me as I played a short but delicate introductory Diego *falseta*. Who knows how I learned it? It must have been those fifteen years of listening.

The first chord of my *siguiriyas* held; dry and terse. Ansonini responded in full voice with a piercing cry. His voice led me on. As soon as the intake of breath was felt and before it was exhaled in its intricate nuance of dissonant tone, it seemed as though I knew on which chord to land. I was there waiting for the landing a split second before it occurred. In a matter of minutes it was impossible to distinguish who was leading and who following. I was flying blind through the darkness of his *cante* supported by the force of his *compás*.

I could smell the cognac on his breath. Is that the smell of age? Cognac on the breath? Or just this one's age? Ansonini smelled like cognac and tears. And let's not mince the truth, cigarettes also. Dark tobacco and all things forbidden.

I moved into the cradle of the *compás* and out again off the A-chord.

I don't know how long we went on together. But when we stopped there was complete silence in the house. As absolute as a coffin. Ansonini and I stared at each other. No one moved and no one spoke. He poured out two glasses of cognac slowly. Then he lifted one glass and set it before me.

"Bebe."

We drank.

"Hombre," he said to me, placing his hand on my knee. He had completely forgotten that I was a woman. "Hombre. Eso es un cuervo blanco. Verdad. Un cuervo blanco.""

"¿Qué dice?" I asked in spite of myself, knowing that this might break the spell. I sensed something enormous had been said and I didn't understand.

"He said your *siguiriyas* was a white raven," said Doug.

"A white raven," I repeated.

"Sí," Ansonini said. We'd never heard Ansonini deliver an explanation of his pronouncements. He exclaimed things as if they were self-evident, and yet this time he went on to explain it.

"We see the raven who is white, we only see it once." Ansonini chuckled, emphatically pouring yet another shot of cognac into my glass.

"She flies before us throughout our lives, though there are many who never see her. Never see her at all. She shows us we can fly blind and with no wings, when the song that is ours is upon us. Your song is *siguiriyas*. Study it every day. Learn its every variation. And this, *niña*, this will carry you through the rest of your life. De verdad." The truth. Ansonini rose from the table, pulled his pants up a bit, looked at all of us and flicked his hand in dismissal. He looked old and tired. The lesson was over.

It all takes so much more time than we think. In spite of the urgency. There is no rushing through the material to move into story. There is no rushing through the scales to move into song.

I have placed pictures of Ansonini at both the beginning and end of my journal. The picture on the inside of the end cover was taken the night before he died. He is beautiful. There is a sadness in his face that seems to lift up off the picture like steam rising up off a lake in an early fall morning. The eyes still burn outwards like small suns burning the fog as the early morning moves along into the day. His gold necklace has not aged as it lies in his grey-white chest hair. And though the medals can't be seen, we know they are there. His patron saint and a silver garlic.

The picture at the start of the journal is one of Ansonini in his early forties. In dungarees and a deep-blue shirt. Near toothless even then. Caught with mouth open. Eyes closed. Arms out like a bird in flight. Dancing.

Chapter 14

I have been in the grips of a voice. All events cluster under the tone. The tone is an A-chord. The shift is to B-flat and back to A. Home is returning to the A.

I once wrote in a letter to Manuel: The world is cold outside of Andalusia. "El mundo es frío fuera de Andalusia. La gente no tiene gracia como tu." The people have no grace like you.

I am afraid depth has a limit. As when we were children and we looked up at the sky and wondered what it meant that the universe had no end. When light travels beyond a certain speed, it begins to move backward in time, they told us. So, too, with thoughts.

This morning I felt that there is history, even in scales. A continuity of time in twelve beats. But where are the notes when we are no longer playing them? And our childhood? Where is our childhood, when we are no longer children?

My father arranged all his shined shoes in the closet in a straight line. And what's more, to me, they appeared to be the same shoes, one after another. He adjusted the small slants and crooked angles he found around the old house every night before he went to bed. And before the plane lifted up off the ground, he would tap the seat three times, crank his neck twice, adjust his pant legs, move his collar around, and lick his two index fingers. When Aaron died he said to me, "I no longer tap my seat three times. It doesn't work. It didn't work."

It's not that Mort didn't see Aaron and me hiding behind the bed as he straightened the shoes. Though he took this gesture seriously, he was lighthearted by nature. And therefore he allowed us to mess up his shoes. For the joke was a good one. But after we left the room and the light from under the door was darkened, we heard. Aaron and I heard him get up again to straighten the shoes. Aaron. My only witness.

That night in the car, outside the Bel Air Hotel. The Porsche. You were in the plum-colored Porsche, the old battered one. What was it you said? "It's not really mine. It's Bernie's. He lent it to me." People were always lending things to you. But Porsches? Big time, big brother. Bernie Feinman's Porsche.

"I'm sorry, Loren," he said. "Really, I can't handle you coming to this party."

"Why not?" I said, feigning a reasonable tone of voice. Desperate inside. Why not? Why can't I come?

"You can't come to this party, Loren. I can't handle it. I'm too fragile. Don't you see? I'm embarrassed for you to meet these people. You're worth a hundred times them. Don't you see? It's all a hype. These things I say. The celebrities. You'd see right through them. There isn't one who can see like you."

"No. I don't see. You're making all this up, to leave me out. It's a new line for the same old cruelty." I was crying. His face, now that I recall it, was lined so deeply. Only thirty. "Aaron, your eyes. Why do they look like that?"

"Loren, don't cry. Christ, can't you understand what I'm saying? There's nothing happening at this party. A bunch of stars. Sniffing coke. Taking drugs. Oh God. I can't handle it. I can't, Loren."

Your profile in the Porsche. Long nose. Receding forehead. Warm eyes. Hands graceful. I got out of the car. There were swans floating down the stream in front of the Bel Air. It was night. The parents were already asleep in their rooms. Safe. You were driving up the curving road to Bernie's house.

I don't believe you. That's the long and short of it. I wake up night after night. My hand over my face. I can't breathe. For a moment you are all different ages. And at every age, I want to come with you.

Naked, Aaron was beautiful. His body was thin, tall, and sturdy. Particularly his arms were beautiful, the muscles in the upper biceps well shaped. If you knew Aaron as well as I did, you would have seen behind the muscles the frail child with teeth chattering. You would have seen the child entering the hard competition of high school, a foot shorter than his classmates, weighing about ninety pounds. You would have seen the thirteen-year-old throwing a tantrum before his bar mitzvah because his head could not be seen over the pulpit where he was to deliver his "Today I am a man" speech while standing on three phone books. You would also have seen me, his sister, standing next to him, 5' 9" tall, one year younger, fully developed, and beautiful. I had only one wish in my mind as I watched my brother's rage. As I watched him kick over the podium, the phone books, and finally deliver a blow to his father's shins. I wished I were three inches shorter than Aaron and ugly.

I am haunted by a photograph of the three of us (me, Aaron, and Mother) in Copenhagen, taken after the family had come to fetch me from the Gypsies. The warmth of Andalusia had suddenly abandoned me as soon as I stepped off the plane in Copenhagen. The cold formality of Scandinavia was so strong that in one moment it overcame three years in Morón under Ansonini's wing. How was that possible? How can protection vanish so quickly?

The picture exposes the triad. Mother stands in the middle, impeccably dressed, with sunglasses from Bergdorf's, her arms around each grown child. Aaron, in profile, is turning away in apparent disinterest. He too wears sunglasses. He's already been in Berkeley one year and has fashionably long hair. He wears a navy blue sweater. An Oxford blue shirt. Faded jeans. He is reading a magazine. He is under tight control, through to an observer he may look composed. I look overweight, La Gorda wearing a thin, worn dress with no shape left. My mother refers to it as "a sack". I stand facing the camera, my face contorted with pain.

Aaron. I dream about you now much less than in the beginning. In the last dream you are alive and we are in the town where we grew up. You are running your fingers through my hair, and then kissing me. You are wearing one earring of mine that Mother gave me. The gold one with the turquoise drop. We are riding a motorcycle. You are driving and it occurs to me that I love you still.

I could write your name on a page five hundred times, and this would not express the number of times I have reconstructed your death. You were found in your house in the Hollywood Hills — nothing sprawling and glamorous. Rather, a little two-story cottage behind a Hollywood house, and built into the edge of a cliff.

Someone said that you had seen God the night before you died. If you did say that, then I can believe you strapped the nitrous mask on. But rather I believe you said it with irony. And if that's the case, then it's possible that someone was there with you who was supposed to take the mask off.

I remember walking into the cottage. First I saw the living room and bedroom. Two steps down to the side was the glassed-in study, where I first saw your long, L-shaped, serious desk. Steps led downstairs from the living room to the kitchen. It was on these steps that you were found. Fallen. The nitrous oxide sitting quietly in the closet upstairs. The body below. The black rubber mask lay where it was casually thrown on the kitchen table next to a small vase with pansies. The gas kept going into the mask, probably with a small but serious hissing sound.

I am convinced that you are dead, though I swear I saw you with my own eyes last week. I accept your presence. I ask if you are afraid. You say no and that you can no longer be distracted from what is at hand. In death you are becoming what you never succeeded at in life. We none of us know what will happen when we give up our ghosts.

Chapter 15

The last time I went to Spain I went on a quest, as some go to Lourdes, to find the wisdom of Santo Diego de Bar Pepe. I would drink of the fountain of his song. The well of his *compás*.

I have been writing my story now for five years. As each of those years came and went, marked by the *compás* of springtime *feria* and the fall harvest *festivales,* I planned my trip back to Andalusia. On the fifth year of the springtime *feria* I decided in one moment to go. In record time, even for a flamenco fanatic, I cleared six months with every possibility to stay longer. I lasted twelve days. And I didn't stay for the *concurso.* The grand contest of the guitar. An unpardonable flamenco sin.

When I arrived I found that "Molly's apartment" had become "Manuel's apartment." An odd twist. I happened upon it this way. I went with Katerina to look at an attic apartment for rent. Though it was at the top of winding stairs, it was charmless. As we looked out the kitchen window a large stork was circling a distant steeple. "Oh," exclaimed Katerina, "that's Manuel's stork. I've never seen him from this side." "How so?" I responded, attempting to keep my passionate curiosity down to casual interest. "Well," she said, "from Manuel's apartment on the other side of the steeple, you can always see the bird circling while you're eating dinner." Even before I knew her, I had heard about Molly's apartment, about how one could be inside and outside at the same time. I had heard stories about how she had had to use an umbrella to go from her bedroom to the kitchen during long rainy winters. I thought to myself, so Molly's apartment has become Manuel's.

That same night it turned out I was more interested in her than in Manuel, but this was as yet undiscovered. I was picked up in Sevilla, straight from the street, and without passing "Go" I was taxied to the Feria of Morón.

I changed clothes in a bar bathroom along the way. This required some thinking. Should I look sexy and spectacular, thereby standing out as clearly non-Gypsy, non-Spanish, an alien from another culture — or should I wear my uniform of many years, the trusty below-the-knee-length faded orange skirt and linen print blouse belted at the waist? The issue of Manuel and the desired impression was tactfully avoided. I decided to look spectacular. After all, this was supposed to be the trip where I maintained my own identity. I put on my black low-cut dress. My Spanish lacework drop earrings and some red lipstick. I was ready to go.

Looking back, it took a kind of courage to dress like that. But at the time I felt a growing uneasiness as I approached Morón. What now looks like courage seemed then like stupidity. Funny how essential qualities of experience can reverse themselves in retrospect. I had begun to wish with all my might that I was wearing my orange skirt. Most of the Americans hanging about the peripheries of the flamenco world looked as Spanish as could be. My dress was a clear statement of modern life. "I live in that other world," I might as well have screamed. That other world all we foreigners pretend does not exist. The one that gives us the money to buy our tickets to come to you.

The lights of the *feria* began to appear in the distance and broke into my self-consciousness. Suddenly I was there. "There" being the edge of the road where the town ended and the lights began. Ferris wheels, carousels, tents, hot *churro* stands and hundreds of people promenading up and down the mile-long strip. It was twelve midnight as the taxi turned and headed back to Sevilla through the darkness. There was nothing to do but to walk forward into the light.

I saw Manuel before he saw me. He stood outside the tent looking nervously about. He looked great. By this I mean it was clear he was loved. Someone had chosen his *camisa*, the shirt fit his spirit like a glove. A black-print linen shirt open at the neck, showing a gold chain. White pants and the traditional black cloth shoes. I suddenly remembered his last postcard to me from Morón: "Hacé mucho frío en la cama sin ti." It is very cold in bed without you. But it was clear even from a distance through all the lights and balloons and candy and activity that Manuel was not *frío en la cama*. I had anticipated every possible reaction except warmth and this is what I received. "¡Lorea! Cómo estás? ¡Qué pasa!" Hugs. Cigarettes. Quick looks. And with no further ado, I entered the *caseta*.

Molly sat with her back to me at a square table with several other women. On the left and right of her were Manuel's two spinster sisters. One with orange hair. One with black. Both close to forty. Other American girls sat also in flowered skirts and blouses. Heavy eye makeup and long earrings. Molly's posture was straight-backed and she did not turn as we walked into the *caseta*. I stayed back at the bar with the men, watching Molly's table. Manuel was off mingling. Like a trout in a stream, this was his element.

I watched Molly, who sat until Manuel approached the table to take her for a promenade. It was in this context that we were reintroduced as if we'd never met. Yet I had known her as a dancer, first come to Sevilla when I walked on Manuel's arm.

And even earlier on, I knew her. When she was a dancer in California, I had played *bulerías* for her lessons. I remembered her in a leotard and long skirt turning round and round in her small basement apartment heated by a wood stove. I was playing a group of sixes over and over as she repeated the steps. She wasn't particularly talented, but she was possessed. This much I have learned to recognize. She was in the grips of a feminine form larger than herself. On one of these turns she would become larger than her life, she hoped. Larger than her job as a waitress. Larger than the small, damp apartment.

She ignored me as do many dancers who hired my services. I don't make sense. I could not be flirted with as foreplay to warm up the *bulerías*. And yet the absence of sexual banter was oddly relieving, as she was free to allow the total vanity and focus that must occur in order to leave the small personal self. She was riveted to the mirror and watched herself unabashedly.

As I watched Molly dance I realized that being a girl matters in this art. It mattered at sixteen and it matters now. Suddenly, and not before, I was alert to that. The book of flamenco commandments says: "Girls dance. Boys play guitar." I had been messing with an archetype and I knew it. Like diving off a high cliff, it was a thrill.

I first met Molly in a formal group dance class. I had been invited by a visiting dancer from Spain to play, along with three men. I dressed like this for the class: Black pants. Silk shirt. And my long black hair up in combs with a small red rose off to one side.

The dancers, beautiful in their high-heeled shoes, leotards, and flowered skirts, jockeyed for position. The American guitarists jockeyed also. They jockeyed around the chairs, casting snide and meaningful looks at each other. The dancers tried to catch their eyes, but the guitarists had eyes only for each other. I humbly took the fourth and last chair to the right of the lead. It was enough for me that several respected Gypsies had publicly announced, "Ella tiene cojones. Más que los hombres americanos." She has balls. More than the American men. Let them put me to the right.

I settled in the uncomfortable straight-backed chair and placed the guitar upright on my knee. Old-style. A position that no doubt contributed to the early demise of many guitarists stronger than I. Originally invented so the guitarist could see the dancer, it became a test of will, requiring a rigidly straight back and an almost inhuman right-hand position.

We were all tuning up. This went on and on. Shifting from the A-chord, employing *bulerías* to the E-chord, indicating *soleares*. There is no way to second-guess which way we will land. One has to be prepared to go either way in a flash — toward joy or toward loneliness. With one foot in each domain, I warmed up my fingers around the essential chords.

The tension was mounting and the dancers were restless, like horses before a storm, their feet alternately tapping sixes and twelves. The room grew suddenly quiet as if on cue, though there had been no exchange of sign. My heart began to race. All eyes moved toward the guitarist on the right and stopped there. He corraled the attention into decision. His hand swung down on the A-chord.

Four guitarists and fifteen dancers rolled into *compás*. Their feet-tapping sounds were bullets that flew past my ears.

I am interested in everyone who has lived out another part of me, and for this reason and no other, Molly haunts me. It seemed fitting and right to be reintroduced. I didn't know her as *la mujer de* Manuel, Manuel's woman, and this certainly was who she had become. Everything about her touched me with compassion. Her thin arms. Her polka-dotted dress with spaghetti straps. Her white, high-heeled shoes. Oh, such effort to belong!

This was not what I had expected. I had been critical and possessive at a distance, from the States. She, after all, was the woman who had replaced me. And she had always been a man's woman. She waited on Manuel's cues. Something I never did. She danced for Manuel's guitar. I wanted to play Manuel's guitar. Yet she had clearly taken on his life. Here was no visitor. Here was a permanent resident.

I was fascinated by her transformation, and I felt my own transformation as a curse. I was no longer Manuel's woman, and as for flamenco, I had barely touched the guitar in three years. I watched Molly all night long, and a long night it was.

The Feria of Morón defies the twenty-four hour day and other such binding physical laws of nature. To begin with, the real night begins at five in the morning after the concert. Manuel was singing through the streets, the arches and the alleyways of Morón. Shutters of apartments flung open as we passed, and what began as curses ended as *"buenos días's"* and *"olé's"* that fell about our heads like small white butter-flies of the morning.

Underneath a particularly magnificent archway hung with vines and purple flowers, Manuel collided with an old village *tonta*. Una *tonta*, a woman simpleton, they are named with affection. He took the scarf from her head and placed it on his own. Same fashion. Tied under his chin. Down he went on his knees and sang to her as loving and lively a *bulerías* as I have ever heard. She began to dance and we began to clap. She joined the promenade, continuing to dance, as we all walked and clapped and sang as we went as a group to the next bar.

At this very bar, already seated, were all the night's performers and their families. And what a list it was! La Fernanda. Ángel and his wife. La Bernarda. Manuel's two sisters and Molly. Our motley group consisted of myself, Katerina, and a few stray aficionados. The dividing line was clear between family and friends. Two more simpletons appeared and joined us.

What happens when you have that much life and art hanging out around a small cluttered table? Cross-eyes. *Tontas. Guasa.* And *cante jondo.* The table erupted. Manuel was still wearing a red scarf tied under his chin. He opened his arms to the group and began his song. The rhythmic clapping began. The guitars came out of their cases. Wine was spilled on the table, ashtrays overflowed onto the floor. Small plates of food kept arriving as if ordered by a nonexistent thoughtful host and the morning and afternoon slid by, the table rocking in *compás* through the smoke-filled haze of the barroom light.

The infamous "day after the fiesta" I stayed in Morón, while Molly hopped the dawn bus back to Sevilla. I thought only to deliver two hundred dollars to Rafael's father, as I had promised him before I left California.

"Place it in his hand only," Rafael had stuttered nervously in his oddly Vietnamese-accented English, which he had learned in his refugee-packed language class. "His hand. His hand only. I don't want my brother-in-law stealing it from him."

I had put off this trip to Spain as long as possible. It would be hard facing Morón again. I felt sadness pulling at my ankles. Did I still belong there? Was it really my world? And so I had asked my friend Alberto to accompany me. He's a dancer who looks more Gypsy than a Gypsy, speaks perfect Andalusian Spanish, complete with bad grammar. The son of Bolivian parents, he grew up in Germany and lives in California, where he dreams of Morón nightly, and longs for his friend Manuel.

And so, Alberto accompanied me. A mistake. Better to have gone alone and let fate deal me what it might. I knew better. Especially in Morón, fate is impossible to avoid. When I'm not being brave, I'm a complete coward. I knew that something was ending.

First and foremost in my mind was to greet Rafael's father. But we were sighted immediately by Manuel on our way past Bar Pepe. And so drinks began in the afternoon. Manuel did not pay particular attention to me, though he was friendly. This might have been a clue. It seemed I'd been through this before, but never one to learn a lesson, not on the first, second, or even third time around, I registered nothing but friendly disinterest as I listened to the men talking as usual at the bar. I have often mistaken withdrawal for disinterest, though I had seen that it can be a preparation for all-out passion.

After an hour or so of small talk, I suggested we visit

Rafael's father. Alberto said sure, but Manuel turned a cold shoulder and declined. He would not, it seemed, even pass by the steps that led up to the old man's *piso*.

"Why?" I asked, knowing no answer would be forthcoming. "You and Rafael have been great childhood friends. He loves you."

Manuel shrugged. The contradictions in Manuel's character would never cease to stump me. He was at once unconditionally kind, warm, and open and, at the same time, shut down, closed, mean. About the darker side of his nature he had no guilt.

Later, Rafael offered his interpretation of Manuel's behavior. He claimed that Manuel would not walk past his one-legged, lame father's house because he, Rafael, had threatened to shoot Manuel's mother when he was last in Morón to attend his own mother's funeral,

"But Manuel's mother has been dead for ten years!" I exclaimed.

"Yes," said Rafael, gleaming maniacally, "that's the point."

The reason that Rafael threatened to shoot Manuel's dead mother is because Manuel refused to go to Rafael's mother's funeral. Why? Because of what Rafael said to Ángel, Manuel's brother, when he was five. Rafael doesn't remember what he said, and that is how the history of the "feud of dead mothers" ends, or should I say, begins. What is all on the inside here, is on the outside there.

Alberto decided to keep the company of Manuel, which was no surprise to me. And so I walked up the stairs to

Rafael's father's house, gratefully alone, to place two hundred dollars in the extraordinarily frail hand.

He was sitting outside the house, four doors up from Bar Pepe, next to my old apartment.

The old man sat in a spot of sun, a very small man with one leg who sold lottery tickets in the market for forty years; since the death of his wife a year ago, he had lost all stamina. He seemed barely a wisp of smoke rising in the hot afternoon as I approached him. I saw that he had become transparent. More air than earth, as old people are before they die. He noticed me only when I was immediately in front of him, his eyes slowly showing recognition.

"Hola. Hola, Lorea. ¿Cómo está mi hijo Rafael y sus niños?"

He took my hand in his and tried to get up to fetch me a chair. I was protesting politely and then avidly, still holding his hand, when a boy appeared quietly at his side. Through the open door I could see the small living room crowded with an overstuffed couch, a table with a vase of artificial flowers, a large picture of the Lord Jesus bleeding on the cross, and a straight-backed chair. The stairway to the second floor, which I knew housed two tiny rooms, was also visible. I remember when the mother of Rafael's young American wife had bought this home. And I remember the whole family moving in. The mother. The father. Rafael and his wife. Three sisters and their numerous children. How they all fit was one of those small pueblo mysteries that an American couldn't even begin to visualize. The texture of their life had been woven with humor, love, vicious argu-

ments, the smell of olive oil and garlic, and music perpetu-
ally springing out of Rafael's manic guitar. Now one of those
babies was eleven years old and he went inside quickly to get
the straight-backed chair for me. He moved again to the old
man's side and put his hand on the transparent shoulder.

"José," I said, calling the boy by name.

He smiled shyly at me with surprise and evident pleasure.
The old man told him my history in a few short phrases as
the boy nodded, his large dark eyes taking in me and my
story with eager interest.

"¿Puedo tener una peseta para un dulce?" he asked me in
his Andalusian Spanish. May I have a penny for a sweet? The
penny in his hand, he was bounding down the stairs, three
at a time, with the old man's chastising rebuke at his heels.

"Está bien. No importa," I said, smiling.

I watched the boy turn the corner and then took my time
watching the street. "Street" is the wrong word. "Alley"
doesn't fit either. There are things that don't translate into
another language and this is one of them. The "street" is
about ten yards wide and it is comprised of hundreds of
stairs and plateaus. At one end is Bar Pepe and at the top of
the steep climb is the park with the bird arboretum. The
street had been renamed Calle Diego del Gastor, Street of
Diego, in honor of the master, who had created his Notre
Dame almost exclusively within the small dark hole which
was and still is Bar Pepe. Now Pepe has died and the new
owner, in an effort to attract the middle class, has lowered
the ceiling, taken down the pictures, and forbidden flamenco. It is a sad joke, for the middle class will never fre-

quent a hole-in-the-wall bar for nothing and discotheques are anyway all the rage in Morón. So the same crowd still hangs out in the hole, but now instead of playing flamenco, they watch it on TV. Priceless pictures and tapes were all moved up to the top of the stairs, where a new flamenco *peña* was built. The *peña* and the view are magnificent, but they couldn't move the gloomy walls of Bar Pepe, and that's where the real history is embedded. If walls could sing!

We sat in the middle of the "street" and I watched the stairs curving in a sweep down to the bar and the small plaza below. I thought my life in this town was like the steps sweeping down below me, each step another dream of my youth. I thought of the few phrases the old man had used to sum up twenty years, and this visit was another step.

He nodded at me. The boy was returning with three pieces of penny candy. This reminded me of Manuel. The young Manuel. Was no gesture, however small, devoid of this resonating train of memories? Manuel sneaking out toward the end of a long nap, and waking me up with small pieces of penny candy placed in my curled moist hand. Penny candy left in special places after small arguments. The penny candy stall in the plaza lit up at night. The pink and yellow wrappers. The child held out his hand. We all three opened our wrappers and popped the nauseatingly sweet candy in our mouths.

It was time to go. The sun had begun to curve past the castle. As I embraced the old man he said to me quietly, "I see Manuel avoid these steps and walk the long way around. He does this every day. Why? I held him as an infant in my arms."

The skinny arms were held out to me as proof. He knew I was a long-standing friend of Manuel's and waited for an explanation. I shrugged. It was all I could do. And he shrugged back, as if to agree with this interpretation. The famous Morón shrug.

I kissed the boy and said take care of the *viejo,* which was unnecessary, as the hand was already back on the frail shoulder. I felt them watching me as I descended back down the steps. A tall American in a faded orange skirt and print blouse.

Manuel and Alberto awaited me at the bar. My shifts of mood were rapidly begining to trouble me and I had no time to weep. This was always a problem in Morón, because weeping was reserved for the music, and I often felt like weeping. Manuel and Alberto and two Spanish friends were deep in conversation about music, and we all went up to Manuel's *piso,* which sits directly next to and upstairs from Bar Pepe. How small is the arena that houses generations of emotion. Not much bigger than a Shakespearean stage.

Entering the large wooden doors of Manuel's piso and gliding up the winding tile stairs of the inner patio after all this time was not just an ordinary act. Oh, no. Not at all. This had been my first home with Manuel, and I had not stepped through its archway in over five years. The men tumbled through the doorway as if it were nothing and while I stood alone staring at the cool inner patio. Alone and feeling small, flooded by memories, I quietly stepped in and up the stairs.

Chapter 16

The first night with Manuel, when I was sixteen years old, before we made love, I urinated in front of him. There was no alternative. The *piso* he lived in, at the top of those winding steps, had no toilet. And yet there was everything we needed next to the bed. A water jug. A bucket to urinate in and a switch that turned on and off the intricate array of wires floating above the bed. One to the TV, another to the radio, another to the light. Let me correct one impression though. The stairs did not wind. That's not exactly it. The huge slabs of tile were placed in a seemingly random order and at angles to each other. These were the steps. Following suit, the floor, made of red tile, was at a sloping, crooked angle also. Before we made love, I had to go to the bathroom. "Aquí está," said Manuel, pointing to the bucket. So I squatted over the bucket. Somehow, after that, making love was less intimidating. The body, already intimate, had nothing to live up to. It was simply a body. The next morning we washed our genitals over a water bucket. That same feeling.

But it was the second time I fell in love with Manuel, my second trip to Spain, when I turned thirty, that leapt into focus as I slowly climbed the stairs.

It was the night of the Gazpacho Festival. For seven years there had been no traditional Gazpacho Festival because the town was mourning Diego's death. Seven years had passed now. Five years since the death of my brother Aaron. And ten years since I had last seen Manuel. This Gazpacho Festival was the town's official end of mourning. Manuel still wore one black button on his grey suit. And I still wore my coat of grief.

I had watched Manuel from nine in the evening until six in the morning. Watched him on stage from a distance, sitting at a table with two Japanese flamenco dancers, an American man who had landed in Morón by accident that evening, and one German aficionado. We all conversed in bad Spanish. I told them nothing of myself, which is something I can easily pull off in a foreign language. In my own language I often feel compelled toward explanation. In fact, the first time Spanish really came onto my ear as an understandable river of words, rather than a jarring collage of half-understood and misunderstood phrases, I was riding in a taxi with Manuel and his brother, speeding through the darkness towards Sevilla for *feria* at twelve midnight.

Manuel and I had napped long and hard. I was alert and relaxed at the same time. Sitting under Manuel's arm in the back of the taxi, I watched the stars which were so large they almost fell through the window. Manuel and Ángel's deep voices were the background noise to this star-watching when suddenly my concentration was broken by unasked-for comprehension. I told no one about it. "¿Qué dice?" I continued to ask.

Same situation now at the table. I don't let on that I've been here before. Or that earlier in the evening I arrived in secret at the bus depot and walked all the old streets up to the plaza and then farther up past the small wall statue of the Virgin, past the houses with ancient wooden windows and up the hill to the crumbling castle. On the way down I had bumped into Manuel's father, who recognized me and remembered my name. I had thought this remembering was a one-way street. It seldom is. He took me to the house and showed me old pictures and then walked with me to the swimming pool where the chairs had been set up for the festival.

I wanted to keep to myself this early evening walk, and so I sat quietly as Manuel took the stage. It was better this way. Seeing him first from a distance. It gave me time to take him in. The balding head. The heavy body. And the same grace-ful movement of the hands. By dawn I was as ready as I would ever be to greet him, unwarned, at the crowded bar.

I hadn't planned to "fall in love" again with Manuel. Not even in fantasy. I had no expectation of the evening, except to walk again through the streets, which had appeared, mag-ical and evasive in their winding, in my dreams for a decade now. That was all. To walk those streets. And when I saw Manuel on stage, so changed was he in appearance that I felt relief at the immediate knowledge that physically I was not drawn. So much for knowledge!

As Manuel turned around to see what child tugged at his suit tails among the noisy festival crowd at the bar, I felt that immediate warmth that I thought I'd never forget or be able to live without, but yet had and did.

"Hola, Lorea," he exclaimed after a moment's pause, his face breaking open. "¿Estás casada?" was the first question he asked after our ten-year separation, going straight to the core.

"Sí," I had responded, mistaking as always that fateful question, "Are you married?" with "¿Estás cansada?", 'Are you tired?.'

Manuel smiled and shaking his head slowly said, "Es una pena." That's unfortunate.

"No," I stammered, catching on. I was always both quick and dumb with the language. "No estoy casada, pero estoy cansada." I'm not married, but I am tired, I said.

"Eso es," Manuel nodded as he took my hand, leading me out of the crowd and onto the road which was just becoming visible in the dawn light. As soon as we were alone on the road, away from the crowded makeshift bar he asked me if I remembered his combing my long black hair on the warm river rocks jutting out from the green pools of rushing water.

"Lo recuerdo," I said. "Recuerdo todo." I remembered the smoke from Ansonini's *potaje*, his one-pot stew, wafting toward us on the breeze. I had felt completely secure with four Gypsy men whose language I didn't understand. We spent the morning driving through small pueblos, picking up bits and pieces for the *potaje*. A chicken here. A tomato there. And then past the last pueblo, over the ancient Roman bridge and onto the secret green pools and rushing stream. The day was hot. And the water cool on the feet. The rock, breast-warm to the body, where we sat. And Manuel, sweet and thin, combing my wet hair and singing a *letra* I was later to understand:

> Péineme con tus peines
> porque tus peines
> son de azúcar

> Comb my hair with your combs
> because your combs
> are made of sugar

This same night, Manuel had peeled shrimp for me, one by one, at a small venta on the road into town. And the same night still or early morning, Manuel — making a hasty retreat from fiesta seekers — had leapt out of the acquired taxi to help fix a flat tire, and had bought a bag of inedible Morón bread, which he used to dry our perspiration.

This time around, still thinking we were "just going to be friends," I was held for hours by his gentle *gracia*, simple charm, and immediate warmth. I felt as always like a child come in to warm small hands against the blazing fire of his soul.

By the time we reached Plaza San Miguel it was ten o'clock strong *de la mañana*. A nasty chill had grown during the early hours and now was radiating from the stone steps of the church where we sat sharing a cigarette.

"¿Tienes frío, niña mia?" Manuel asked, holding my face in both his hands. Are you cold, child of mine?

"¿Tienes frío, niña mia?" he said again, putting his arm around me and pulling me close in.

"¿Tienes frío?" he repeated, placing my head on his chest as he began to rock me, saying over and over, "¿Tienes frío, niña mia? . . . ¿Tienes frío, niña mia?"

"Tengo frío. . . . Tengo frío," I responded in a singsong chant as we rocked together. I am cold. I am cold. And my body, which had been so cold for so long after Aaron's death, opened again, in that ancient and foreign place.

Chapter 17

The wall across from Manuel's *piso* has been painted
white. Still though, the doves come, as they have for the past
thousand years. The room also has been painted white.
There is furniture now. A dark wood table with four heavy,
straight-backed chairs. A straight-backed couch for two.
And a bookshelf with assorted tapes, pictures, and a tape
recorder instead of books. The pictures of me are gone from
the walls. The door to the second room is slightly ajar with
the unmade bed visible. It is the same room where Manuel
and his three brothers and two sisters were raised. The same
room where, five years ago and ten years before that, we
lived together. Other women have also lived here with
Manuel. But somehow this is not a disturbing thought. I
don't feel possessive of this man. Never have. When asked by
a former girlfriend whom he loved best of all his women,
he answered, "I loved them all best." And Manuel has
this capacity. To be indiscriminate in love. Manuel, the
umbrella fixer. Manuel, the walking hearth.

A group of men are sitting in Manuel's piso smoking cigarettes and listening to the *cante*. They have hardly taken notice of me as I quietly enter the room. It is a mixture of grief and insult, this constant ignoring that goes on in any group of Gypsy men. I don't exist. Yet I know they are acutely aware as I cross my legs. Vigilant of the hem of my skirt.

"¿Quieres un cigarro?" is how Manuel notices me, and then back to an explanation of Antonio Mairena, who is singing *bulerías* on an old and beloved tape.

Manuel begins to clap *palmas* to further elucidate his explanation. His whole body becomes involved. The foot stamps on the three. The head nods on the accent. The eyebrows lift in anticipation. The torso leans forward as the *cante* drives home its meaning. All the men in the room move forward with him. I also move. This is an extraordinary lesson in listening. The whole room leans. The bookshelves, the chairs, and the walls lean also, as Manuel accents the last three beats and pronounces "¡Olé!" with a definitive nod of his head. "¡Olé!" we all pronounce in agreement and the room moves back to perpendicular lines with men sitting in straight-backed chairs. *Gusto* resonates as the men nod at each other, pass around the sherry, exchange a few small words, and begin again this journey of listening.

I never understood the appeal of solo flamenco guitar, I think of saying, but don't. There is nothing to compare to those feet and hands pounding out rhythms of *compás*. I don't get *"olé's"* after every sentence that I write. Nor do I have a supporting *compás* for each paragraph. Yet I must continue. Alone. Like the solo guitarist. I am jealous of Manuel. This is new. I want my own *"olé's."* I sigh.

"¿Quieres algo?" Manuel asks, hearing my sigh. Do you want something?

"Sí, un cigarro," I say.

I remembered the moment, listening to *soleares,* when I thought: *falsetas* are infinite. There are enough of these that learning them all would last a lifetime. They could never run out, and they didn't. I did. I cross my legs twice in rapid succession. I light up a cigarette and sigh much too loudly. This breaks the listening trance.

"¿Qué, niña?" Manuel asks with an edge of irritation this time and a movement of the hand out into the air.

"Tengo hambre," I explain. "No he comido desde la mañana, Manuel." I'm hungry.

This is understood and accepted among the group as a good enough reason to break up and reconvene at the *peña* for a meal. I shake hands with the two friends, and Manuel, Alberto and I walk slowly down the stairs, out into what is now the night and up the many hundred steps to the *peña.* I try to explain to Alberto that my mood has shifted radically in a direction I don't understand. I have fallen out of *compás,* I tell him. I need to go home. He ignores me and refuses to understand, as if he were a Spanish man.

Like mercury, Alberto changes his character when he gets anywhere within a hundred yards of Manuel. He can't help it. It was all those years growing up in Germany with the face of a Bolivian peasant. He's never belonged to any culture and here, with Manuel, he is at peace. I know this about

Alberto and now it seems blindness on my part to have taken him with me. I would have been better off alone. "It's just temporary," Alberto encourages me, generously condescending to say this in English. I know that he is wrong.

The three of us sit down outside. Manuel orders dinner for all of us. The park, and then the lights of the town, and then darkness, stretch out before us. We can feel the presence of the ruined castle and the outline of the mountains around the town, though it is too dark to see. The stars are falling into the darkness around the town as if we were on an island surrounded by the ocean. The food begins to arrive, and along with it several friends from town, including a couple our own age. They are all invited to join the table. The talk turns to the bullfight of yesterday when a young hero of Spain was killed. The bull was killed in reprisal and this was much under debate. That day, fifty thousand people in Sevilla had walked behind the coffin to the home of the young matador's fiancée, where she and her family had joined the procession and continued on to the cemetery. The conversation is heated. Opinions flying. I notice that the other Spanish woman from Morón is not talking either. My efforts to strike up a conversation with her go nowhere. I look to the stars again and let the conversation drift out of my understanding. That is easy to do in a foreign language. Once you lose a couple of sentences, you can be whole topics behind. And so I am taken by surprise when the whole group rises to go inside.

Manuel is again explaining a point. I finally pick up the conversation and realize that a specific move made by the matador before his death is under close scrutiny. We're all in the large fiesta room sitting around a table. Evidently the chill in the air has brought us inside. The waiters bring the remaining tapas from outside and a new round of drinks is ordered. Now we are seven; the three of us, the young couple from Morón, and the two men in their fifties — cement factory workers, who had been with us earlier in Manuel's *piso*.

Manuel rises from the table to emphasize his point. Suddenly he grabs a red tablecloth from an empty table. He draws it around his hips and ties a knot. He carefully folds another tablecloth over a broom so that the cloth hangs in perfect folds like a matador's cape. This done, he stands at attention and motions to Alberto.

"Dame palmas. Bulerías, por favor."

Alberto begins to clap out the *bulerías*. He is really excellent at this. Alberto's *palmas* can make him look and sound more Spanish than a Spaniard. The other men join with counterrhythm. Manuel moves into his motions so precisely and with such dignity, it almost seems like an instant replay in slow motion. I am gripped along with the others at the table.

"Como así," he explains as he baits the imaginary bull, moving slowly in *compás* to the rhythm. He holds our attention completely, and then suddenly he breaks into a turn, in *compás*, cape flying, and out the other side.

"Así!" he exclaims amid the *"olé's"* and *"viva-tu's."* "¡Así! ¡Así!" as he points his cape at the bull.

It doesn't take a seasoned aficionado to know that we are witnessing an event of complete originality. Over and over,

Manuel dances out each play of the death that was discussed all evening. We can hear the yells of the crowd. We can see fifty thousand umbrellas opening at once, as the rain suddenly starts. Manuel begins urging Alberto to be the bull. Finally he can hold out no longer and joins Manuel's death-defying dance of *bulerías* with as much seriousness as Manuel. The clapping continues on and on, as the two men dance with each other in absolute dignity and *compás*.

I feel the death. Yet it is my own, and not the young matador's. There they are, two men dancing before me. I am distracted. I am losing my own voice in the twelve beats. I am going under, and for the first time I want to stay afloat. I fight against it.

"Quiero ir," I say to Manuel in the very midst of his turn. I want to go.

"Quiero ir," I repeat loudly as the clapping stops, and Manuel looks at me, stunned.

But this day that had been going nonstop was still not over. I nervously fingered my ancient Jewish star, found in the Barrio Santa Cruz, as Alberto and Manuel walked me to the Pensión Pasqual. I desperately urged Manuel to call a taxi so I could return to Sevilla. I felt I had disrupted enough. But it was two in the morning and he would not hear of it. Still the gentleman and still in charge of the three of us, he made a detour up the castle road to a small, open bar and ordered yet another meal for all of us. "This is not happening," his gestures said. "You are as close to me as ever." Did he realize I was not? I don't know, but in my sudden, unexpected disruption of his *gusto* was the hidden fantasy we both had that maybe we could still be together after all. Perhaps the separation had been a sad mistake, his five years with Molly and my five years back in California. This unspoken thought had been building in us both during the evening. My interruption put an end to that harmless but tenacious fantasy. A deep sadness overcame the table and stayed with us as Alberto and Manuel walked me to the pension.

That night I dreamt about Manuel and Molly. In the dream they were stepping onto what appeared to be a bus in Sevilla. But really they had climbed onto carousel horses that were suspended over a bridge of lights that spanned Sevilla. City of daydreams, of hidden fountains, of quiet candles in darkened churches. Manuel turned around and waved to me. A sad slow wave. Goodbye, I said. Goodbye. I felt my childhood departing. Then I was alone.

On our last morning together, sadness hung over us like early morning mist. The change in me eluded him. And we somehow avoided the cause of my sudden departure as if it didn't exist.

My train left at six in the morning and Manuel had offered to go with me to the station. The sun appeared to be a nervous orange rising over the surface of the aging city as we walked through the streets and crossed the Triana bridge. I told him about the white raven, but I could not be sure that he understood.

We wandered aimlessly through the station, whose arches and lacework canopies remained exactly as they were at conception and on any normal day would fill the heart with the magic of trains. We found my train, El Torre de Oro, puffing and steaming in its place, preparing for departure, and I climbed aboard. Neither of us protested. I felt emptied. I had fallen out of *compás*.

The train whistle blew and blew as the train wrenched itself out of its Sevilla home. I kept my head turned back in an effort to catch my last view of the city dawn and of Manuel standing quietly, until the train, gaining speed, jerked my head around and forward.

As I turned away from Sevilla I begin to imagine the white walls of my studio, thousands of miles away. I see a long, white, L-shaped desk, and now I know it is my turn to play.

The first chord of my *siguiriyas* holds: dry and terse. There is shuffling in the space around me and the familiar, stunned, is sent to the corners as the tracks of my dead stretch out before me — or are they the grooves, deep and wet, that run down the sides of Ansonini's face? The white dust of bone knocking against bone settles on my fingernails. From Ansonini's toothless mouth the wind is emanating. I can smell the age of his skin and the lines in his face are rivers I am traveling. A consciousness comes out of stone. A weeping moves in from the outside. My *falseta* flies out over the darkening earth.

–END–

HOMAGE TO DIEGO DEL GASTOR
by Christopher Carnes

Christopher Carnes plays solo Spanish flamenco guitar in the Gypsy tradition of spontaneous improvisation, inspired by his teacher, Diego del Gastor.

This 45-minute audio tape, a companion to *Returning to A,* is available from City Lights Mail Order, 261 Columbus Avenue, San Francisco, CA 94133. $9.95, plus $3.00 shipping charge.

Glossary

Aficionados Flamenco aficionados are knowledgeable listeners. They are professionals as well as amateurs and are necessary for a good fiesta.

Aire A particular quality a flamenco guitarist brings to his art. *"Tiene aire"* means "it swings" as you would say of jazz.

Alegrías A *cante chico* form that embodies a happy and light-hearted feeling. Unlike the *soleares,* its chords are in the major key.

Baile Flamenco dance.

Bulerías The flamenco form that occupies a special and supreme position at the heart of the fiesta. It is the most flexible form; constantly changing, spontaneous, full of humor, and yet majestic.

Caló Caló is the Spanish dialect of the Gypsy language. It can be traced directly to India through its Sanscrit roots. Caló is essentially a dead language although it is still known by the older generation of Gypsies. Certain phrases and words appear in flamenco verse.

Cante; cante Flamenco singing; a particular flamenco song.

Cante chico Light songs, which are more danceable, more accessible, and brighter. They express gay, lively, whimsical feelings. They include rhumbas, tangos, and *alegrías.*

Cante jondo Deep song refers to forms that express profound feelings, such as loneliness tragedy, loss.

Caseta A small tent or house constructed as a temporary party place for families or groups of families and friends during *ferias.*

Compás A repetitive rhythmic pattern with accents falling on specific beats. *Compás* is the primary defining feature of a flamenco form.

Duende	Originally, the little spirits that inhabit farm houses. In flamenco it has come to mean the expression of soul, another presence that enters into the artist and transforms expression.
Falseta	A melody played on the flamenco guitar. *Falsetas* can be original spontaneous improvisations or they can be learned and traditional.
Festero	A person whose spirit is a catalyst for a fiesta. Often an expert at *bulerías*.
Golpe	A right-handed rhythmic tap on top of the guitar.
Letra	A flamenco verse to be sung. These include *cante jondo* and *cante chico*. They are sometimes anonymous, sometimes attributed to a certain singer. On rare occasions they are improvised. They are passed down from one generation to the next.
Palmas	Rhythmic hand-clapping accompaniment.
Piso	An apartment or flat.
Picado	A guitar technique utilizing alternating first and second fingers of the right hand.
Rasgueado	A right-handed strumming technique that supports the *compás*.
Siguiriyas	Considered the most *jondo* of all the flamenco forms, it expresses personal tragedy from which there is no relief or escape.
Soleares, soleá	Derived from *soledad*, loneliness. The verse in *soleares* often expresses nostalgia for love lost, and for one's separateness; a single song in this form.
Toque	Refers to a particular style, such as *soleares*, or to an artist's life work (i.e., the *toque* of Diego del Gastor).

For further exposition of *cante jondo* and *duende*, see *Deep Song and Other Essays* by Federico García Lorca. For more complete definitions of flamenco forms, see *The Art of Flamenco* by Don Pohren.

Acosta, Juvenal, ed. LIGHT FROM A NEARBY WINDOW:
Contemporary Mexican Poetry
Alberti, Rafael. CONCERNING THE ANGELS
Alcalay, Ammiel, ed. KEYS TO THE GARDEN: New Israeli Writing
Allen, Roberta. AMAZON DREAM
Angulo de, G. & J. JAIME IN TAOS
Artaud, Antonin. ARTAUD ANTHOLOGY
Bataille, Georges. EROTISM: Death and Sensuality
Bataille, Georges. THE IMPOSSIBLE
Bataille, Georges. STORY OF THE EYE
Bataille, Georges. THE TEARS OF EROS
Baudelaire, Charles. TWENTY PROSE POEMS
Blake, N., Rinder, L., & A. Scholder, eds. IN A DIFFERENT LIGHT:
Visual Culture, Sexual Culture, Queer Practice
Blanco, Alberto. DAWN OF THE SENSES: Selected Poems
Bowles, Paul. A HUNDRED CAMELS IN THE COURTYARD
Bramly, Serge. MACUMBA: The Teachings of Maria-José, Mother of the Gods
Brook, J. & Iain A. Boal. RESISTING THE VIRTUAL LIFE:
Culture and Politics of Information
Broughton, James. COMING UNBUTTONED
Broughton, James. MAKING LIGHT OF IT
Brown, Rebecca. ANNIE OAKLEY'S GIRL
Brown, Rebecca. THE TERRIBLE GIRLS
Bukowski, Charles. THE MOST BEAUTIFUL WOMAN IN TOWN
Bukowski, Charles. NOTES OF A DIRTY OLD MAN
Bukowski, Charles. TALES OF ORDINARY MADNESS
Burroughs, William S. THE BURROUGHS FILE
Burroughs, William S. THE YAGE LETTERS
Cassady, Neal. THE FIRST THIRD
CITY LIGHTS REVIEW #2: AIDS & the Arts
CITY LIGHTS REVIEW #3: Media and Propaganda
CITY LIGHTS REVIEW #4: Literature / Politics / Ecology
Cocteau, Jean. THE WHITE BOOK (LE LIVRE BLANC)
Cornford, Adam. ANIMATIONS
Corso, Gregory. GASOLINE
Cuadros, Gil. CITY OF GOD
Daumal, René. THE POWERS OF THE WORD
David-Neel, Alexandra. SECRET ORAL TEACHINGS IN TIBETAN
BUDDHIST SECTS
Deleuze, Gilles. SPINOZA: Practical Philosophy
Dick, Leslie. KICKING
Dick, Leslie. WITHOUT FALLING
di Prima, Diane. PIECES OF A SONG: Selected Poems
Doolittle, Hilda (H.D.). NOTES ON THOUGHT & VISION
Ducornet, Rikki. ENTERING FIRE
Duras, Marguerite. DURAS BY DURAS

Eberhardt, Isabelle. DEPARTURES: Selected Writings
Eberhardt, Isabelle. THE OBLIVION SEEKERS
Eidus, Janice. VITO LOVES GERALDINE
Fenollosa, Ernest. CHINESE WRITTEN CHARACTER AS A MEDIUM
    FOR POETRY
Ferlinghetti, L. ed. THE CITY LIGHTS POCKET POETS ANTHOLOGY
Ferlinghetti, L., ed. ENDS & BEGINNINGS (City Lights Review #6)
Ferlinghetti, Lawrence. PICTURES OF THE GONE WORLD
    (Enlarged 1995 edition)
Finley, Karen. SHOCK TREATMENT
Ford, Charles Henri. OUT OF THE LABYRINTH: Selected Poems
Franzen, Cola, transl. POEMS OF ARAB ANDALUSIA
García Lorca, Federico. BARBAROUS NIGHTS: Legends & Plays
García Lorca, Federico. ODE TO WALT WHITMAN & OTHER POEMS
García Lorca, Federico. POEM OF THE DEEP SONG
Gil de Biedma, Jaime. LONGING: SELECTED POEMS
Ginsberg, Allen. THE FALL OF AMERICA
Ginsberg, Allen. HOWL & OTHER POEMS
Ginsberg, Allen. KADDISH & OTHER POEMS
Ginsberg, Allen. MIND BREATHS
Ginsberg, Allen. PLANET NEWS
Ginsberg, Allen. PLUTONIAN ODE
Ginsberg, Allen. REALITY SANDWICHES
Goethe, J. W. von. TALES FOR TRANSFORMATION
Harryman, Carla. THERE NEVER WAS A ROSE WITHOUT A THORN
Hayton-Keeva, Sally, ed. VALIANT WOMEN IN WAR AND EXILE
Heider, Ulrike. ANARCHISM: Left Right & Green
Herron, Don. THE DASHIELL HAMMETT TOUR: A Guidebook
Herron, Don. THE LITERARY WORLD OF SAN FRANCISCO
Higman, Perry, tr. LOVE POEMS FROM SPAIN AND SPANISH AMERICA
Jaffe, Harold. EROS: ANTI-EROS
Jenkins, Edith. AGAINST A FIELD SINISTER
Katzenberger, Elaine, ed. FIRST WORLD, HA HA HA!
Kerouac, Jack. BOOK OF DREAMS
Kerouac, Jack. POMES ALL SIZES
Kerouac, Jack. SCATTERED POEMS
Kerouac, Jack. SCRIPTURE OF THE GOLDEN ETERNITY
Lacarrière, Jacques. THE GNOSTICS
La Duke, Betty. COMPAÑERAS
La Loca. ADVENTURES ON THE ISLE OF ADOLESCENCE
Lamantia, Philip. MEADOWLARK WEST
Laughlin, James. SELECTED POEMS: 1935–1985
Laure. THE COLLECTED WRITINGS
Le Brun, Annie. SADE: On the Brink of the Abyss
Mackey, Nathaniel. SCHOOL OF UDHRA
Masereel, Frans. PASSIONATE JOURNEY
Mayakovsky, Vladimir. LISTEN! EARLY POEMS
Mrabet, Mohammed. THE BOY WHO SET THE FIRE

Mrabet, Mohammed. THE LEMON
Mrabet, Mohammed. LOVE WITH A FEW HAIRS
Mrabet, Mohammed. M'HASHISH
Murguía, A. & B. Paschke, eds. VOLCAN: Poems from Central America
Murillo, Rosario. ANGEL IN THE DELUGE
Parenti, Michael. AGAINST EMPIRE
Pasolini, Pier Paolo. ROMAN POEMS
Pessoa, Fernando. ALWAYS ASTONISHED
Peters, Nancy J., ed. WAR AFTER WAR (City Lights Review #5)
Poe, Edgar Allan. THE UNKNOWN POE
Porta, Antonio. KISSES FROM ANOTHER DREAM
Prévert, Jacques. PAROLES
Purdy, James. THE CANDLES OF YOUR EYES
Purdy, James. GARMENTS THE LIVING WEAR
Purdy, James. IN A SHALLOW GRAVE
Purdy, James. OUT WITH THE STARS
Rachlin, Nahid. THE HEART'S DESIRE
Rachlin, Nahid. MARRIED TO A STRANGER
Rachlin, Nahid. VEILS: SHORT STORIES
Reed, Jeremy. DELIRIUM: An Interpretation of Arthur Rimbaud
Reed, Jeremy. RED-HAIRED ANDROID
Rey Rosa, Rodrigo. THE BEGGAR'S KNIFE
Rey Rosa, Rodrigo. DUST ON HER TONGUE
Rigaud, Milo. SECRETS OF VOODOO
Ross, Dorien. RETURNING TO A
Ruy Sánchez, Alberto. MOGADOR
Saadawi, Nawal El. MEMOIRS OF A WOMAN DOCTOR
Sawyer-Lauçanno, Christopher, transl. THE DESTRUCTION OF THE JAGUAR
Scholder, Amy, ed. CRITICAL CONDITION: Women on the Edge of Violence
Sclauzero, Mariarosa. MARLENE
Serge, Victor. RESISTANCE
Shepard, Sam. MOTEL CHRONICLES
Shepard, Sam. FOOL FOR LOVE & THE SAD LAMENT OF PECOS BILL
Smith, Michael. IT A COME
Snyder, Gary. THE OLD WAYS
Solnit, Rebecca. SECRET EXHIBITION: Six California Artists
Sussler, Betsy, ed. BOMB: INTERVIEWS
Takahashi, Mutsuo. SLEEPING SINNING FALLING
Turyn, Anne, ed. TOP TOP STORIES
Tutuola, Amos. FEATHER WOMAN OF THE JUNGLE
Tutuola, Amos. SIMBI & THE SATYR OF THE DARK JUNGLE
Valaoritis, Nanos. MY AFTERLIFE GUARANTEED
Veltri, George. NICE BOY
Wilson, Colin. POETRY AND MYSTICISM
Wilson, Peter Lamborn. SACRED DRIFT
Wynne, John. THE OTHER WORLD
Zamora, Daisy. RIVERBED OF MEMORY